ENIGMATIC ECHOES

SERIES BY NELLIE H. STEELE

Cate Kensie Mysteries
Shadow Slayers Stories
Lily & Cassie by the Sea Mysteries
Pearl Party Mysteries
Middle Age is Murder Cozy Mysteries
Duchess of Blackmoore Mysteries
Maggie Edwards Adventures
Clif & Ri on the Sea Adventures
Shelving Magic
Whispers of Witchcraft

This is a work of fiction. Names, characters, places, and incidents either are the product of the author's imagination or are used fictitiously. Any resemblance to actual persons, living or dead, events, or locales is entirely coincidental.

Copyright © 2024 by Nellie H. Steele

All rights reserved.

No part of this book may be reproduced in any form or by any electronic or mechanical means, including information storage and retrieval systems, without written permission from the author, except for the use of brief quotations in a book review.

Cover design by Stephanie A. Sovak.

❦ Created with Vellum

ENIGMATIC ECHOES

WHISPERS OF WITCHCRAFT
BOOK FOUR

NELLIE H. STEELE

CHAPTER 1

My eyes slid sideways toward my enigmatic grandmother as we made our return trip home. She'd promised me another story, this one in Scotland and directly relating to the music box I'd fallen in love with when I'd arrived at Thornwood Manor.

Supposedly, the music box had come from one of Emma's adventures. But I was starting to suspect Emma wasn't a friend of my grandmother's but was actually my grandmother herself.

I hadn't said anything to her yet about my idea. I wondered if maybe she'd laugh at me. But more than that, I wondered why, if she was Emma, why would she have kept it from me.

Why not just say she was the one who had all these weird experiences.

Maybe she thought I'd laugh at her.

After what she'd told me about how many spirits Emma and Rose had helped so far, I wouldn't laugh. In fact, I'd be in awe if it was her who had done all this. She must have lived a really interesting life.

Far more interesting than what I'd lived so far, growing up in an area that prized fitting into a mold rather than being unique.

As much as I missed my parents, coming to live with my grandmother had been a blessing in disguise.

"Are you excited to get home?" she asked after a while.

"Yeah," I answered, pulling my mind from my whirlwind of thoughts to the present. "It was fun to see new things though."

"Well, we have plenty more to plan, don't we?" My grandmother grinned as she studied the road ahead. "Maybe next time you can drive."

"Really?" I asked, my eyes going wide.

"Well, you've got to get your permit and learn, but…every young woman should know how to navigate around and explore on her own."

"Mom always said we shouldn't go too far on our own."

"Nonsense." She slid her eyes sideways to me. "What you should be, though, is prepared. Both mentally and physically. The world can be an unkind place, Carly."

"I think that's why Mom and Dad never really let me go exploring."

"Oh, but you should. With pepper spray and a self-defense class."

I giggled at her. "I'd like to learn self-defense, actually."

"Oh, good. I'll get lessons arranged. And I wondered… what would you say about home-schooling instead of going to a school? It's your choice and we have a few months to decide. We can tour the schools first if you'd like. There's the Midnight Hollow Public School, of course, and the Academy."

I wondered if they were anything different from my school when I lived on Lilac Lane. I didn't like my school very much, though I did have some friends. "I'd like to think about it."

"Yes, absolutely," Grandmother said as we sped down the road. "And we should discuss it at length. There is no right answer, Carly. Only the right answer for you."

"That's a good thought," I said with a bob. "If more people thought that way…"

"The world would be a far kinder, happier place. Too many people decide things for others."

"But isn't it being selfish to decide it for yourself?"

She glanced at me as we came to a stop at a light in the center of a small town. "Heavens no. Are you going to harm anyone if you choose to go to the Academy instead of home school or vice versa?"

I shrugged. "I guess not."

"Then you are not being selfish. Selfish is when you make the wrong choices for the wrong reasons because eventually you will not be able to sustain them."

"Hmm, I never thought of it like that. Okay, I'll give the schools some thought. I kind of like the idea of being home schooled because– "

"Don't say you'll have less work because you will likely have more. I'm no pushover," Grandmother warned.

"I was going to say it could be more tailored to my interests and also more flexible."

"Yes, it is that. We could travel and do your schooling. But don't take it for that reason only. We can work around your schedule if you'd like to go to class with other young people your age."

"Hmm, I'll see. I don't get along with a lot of young people my age."

Grandmother laughed as we passed through the tree-lined streets of Midnight Hollow. "I never did either. I was a bit of a loner."

I shifted in my seat as I considered asking her about what I'd seen on her license, but before I could, the town faded behind us.

"Here we are," she said as we turned onto our road. "I'm certain Whiserkina will be pleased to be able to run all over the house."

"I'll bet," I said with a nod as I ruffled the fur on my new kitten's head.

We rumbled down the drive with Lester waving at us from his perch trimming a tree and arrived at the house.

"We can start planning our next trip over dinner if you'd like."

"Actually, I'd really like to hear about Scotland. Can we plan the next trip starting tomorrow?"

"Of course. I'm so pleased you enjoy my stories."

I bobbed my head with a smile as we climbed from the car and gathered our things. "I do. And I'm dying to hear about this music box. It's so unique."

"And we'll have to find a spot for the one you found in that resale shop."

My mind returned to the sea-themed music box and locket I'd found. I'd felt a strange pull toward it, almost like I couldn't stop myself from studying it. I wondered if I'd feel the same way when I saw it again after I unwrapped it from the careful packaging. "Yeah. I can't wait to see it again. I keep wondering if I thought it was more special in the store than it actually was."

"Oh, no, I think you'll find it has the same appeal here as in the store."

We carried our things into the house. I set Whiskerina down to scamper around as I carried my bags up the stairs to my bedroom and dumped them on the bed.

I'd unpack in a minute, but first I wanted to see the music box I'd bought.

I plopped onto the bed and tugged the wrapped items from the bag. First, I unwrapped the locket that opened the music box, then tackled the paper around the bronze box. My fingertips ran over the carvings of mermaids and anchors that covered it.

I set it on the bed and grabbed the locket emblazoned with the woman's profile. Pressing it into the indentation on the front of the box, the top popped open. A delicate mermaid danced inside as the melancholic melody played.

When I'd touched the mermaid's tiny hand in the store, it had shocked me. I wondered if it would do the same now. I reached for it, but before my finger connected with her porcelain hand, a knock startled me.

"Come in!" I yelled.

My door creaked open, and my grandmother hovered inside. "Well, you're right where I expected you'd be. And does the little box have the same appeal as it did in the store?"

I grinned at her as I bobbed my head. "Yep. Now, to find a spot to put it."

"Why not put it next to the other for now. But I had a thought."

"What?" I asked as I carried it over, setting it next to my Scottish music box.

"Well, you seem to love music boxes. I'd imagine during our travels, you may pick up more. Perhaps Lester can place some shelves for you to display them. Or maybe a curio. We could put it here in the corner."

"Oh, that would be nice," I said. "But not one of those modern glass ones. Can we find one that's wood with carvings?"

"Yes," she answered with a smile, "let's plan on doing some antiquing soon. We may find something like that in one of the shops."

"Okay. And I was going to unpack...I was just excited to see my find."

"Of course, you were. I'm merely here to tell you that it seems the weather will cooperate with our plans for storytelling tonight."

I glanced out the window at the sunny day. "Really? It looks nice out."

"Well, Lester has told me he's pleased we are home because there are bad storms coming around dinner time."

I bounced on my toes, barely able to contain my excitement. "Ohh, boy! More scary stories with a storm in the background."

"Yes. I'm going to get a start on the dinner and treats for afterward. We can drink homemade hot chocolate by the fire as you hear the first bits about Velvet Manor."

"Velvet Manor?" I repeated. "It sounds...posh."

"Oh, it was a grand place. Hidden amidst the fog-laden moors. Absolutely fabulous." She flicked a knowing glance my way. "We really should plan an overseas trip because if you thought Maple Manor was grand, you'd be stunned with this spot."

"Wow. I'd love to. I've never been out of the country. But...you've been, right?"

"Oh, yes. I've traveled all over the world. It's quite an experience. And I'd very much like for you to have it, too."

"Well, I can't wait to hear about it, and hopefully I'll have my own experiences, too. I'll unpack and then come down and help you with dinner."

"All right," she said with a nod before she stepped into the hall. "See you soon."

I hurried around my room, pulling my clothes from my bag and returning them to their drawers or the closet. I had the task finished in no time.

With my Scottish music box in hand, I raced downstairs

and into the kitchen. My grandmother hovered over her slow cooker, stirring the little piece of chocolate heaven we'd have for dessert.

"Can I do anything?" I asked as I slid the music box onto the counter.

"Yes. Why don't you shred up the lettuce? I thought we may prefer something light, so I've made a strawberry salad."

"Mmm, that sounds good." I crossed to the opposite counter and grabbed the already-cleaned lettuce, tearing it apart and filling the bowl.

Lester pushed through the back door across the room, his shirt speckled with dark spots. "Already starting to rain," he announced.

"Just in time for our story."

"Which one are we on?" he asked.

"Velvet Manor," my grandmother said as she chopped strawberries.

"Oh, Scotland." Lester's eyebrows shot up as he grinned. "That's a good one."

"So, have you heard all of my grandmother's stories?"

"Most of them," he answered with a nod. "Each one better than the last. You're in for a treat with this one. And if I'm not mistaken, your music box came from Velvet Manor."

"You are correct, Lester," Grandmother said.

The first rumble of thunder clapped overhead. "Well, I'll go ready the fire."

"Excellent. I propose we eat in front of it. It will be appropriate for the start of this story."

I tugged my lips back in an excited grin as I bounced on my toes.

We finished the meal preparations and, salads in hand, made our way to the living room. Rain already pelted the roof and thunder continued to growl. I tossed a throw pillow on the floor and plopped onto it as Lester and my grandmother eased into the armchairs near the fireplace.

Whiskerina climbed into my cross-legged seat and curled into a ball.

After my first bite, I said, "Okay, I can't wait any longer. Can we start the story now?"

My grandmother grinned at me and bobbed her head. "Yes. I humbly present Veils of Velvet Manor."

Emma squinted through the windshield, desperately trying to see through the fog that surrounded her and Rose's car as they slowly crept down the narrow road.

Rose fiddled with the map, tracing a finger along a squiggly line. "I don't know. I think we're close."

"I guess they couldn't make it easy to find," Emma answered, ducking to survey more of the landscape. "What is with this fog?"

"Welcome to Scotland," Rose answered.

"I was hoping for a sunnier welcome," Emma answered as a dark object loomed on the horizon. "Oh, wait, I think I see something."

"That makes one of us. Thank goodness we already stopped for groceries. I wouldn't want to be out in this soup."

"Thanks for coming with me," Emma answered as she reached for her aunt's hand. "I'm glad to have someone to bounce ideas off of and read the map."

Rose squeezed her hand. "You're welcome. And, yes, I think we've made it."

Emma aimed for the sprawling, dark mansion rising from the fog-laden moors. A gravel drive led from the main road to the gothic structure.

She eased the car to a stop, her eyes lingering on it. "Well, it certainly looks *haunted."*

Rose chuckled as she flung her door open and wrapped her

sweater tighter around her as the misty air floated into the car. "They all look haunted. The question is, are they really?"

"Well, this has been abandoned for at least a few months, the owner said. No one wanted to stay here with all the disturbances." Emma slung the strap of her bag over her shoulder before she hefted a few grocery bags onto her hips.

"Shall we give it a go?" Rose asked, grabbing the remaining two bags.

"Yep. The owner said it would be unlocked. Said no one will come near the place."

Emma crossed to the door and fiddled with the knob before she flung it open. With a deep breath, she stepped into the dusty foyer, her footsteps echoing on the ornate wooden floor.

The high, domed ceiling drew her eyes up the sweeping, curved staircase to the next floor.

"Wow," Rose answered, her voice echoing off the walls. "This place is something."

"Yes," Emma murmured.

"Getting anything?" Rose asked.

"Oh, yes. This house is haunted, all right. By more than one ghost."

CHAPTER 2

"Wow," I said, my eyes going wide. "She knew right away?"

My grandmother set her plate aside as she nodded. "Oh, yes. This presence was quite strong. Quite strong, indeed."

The way her eyebrows pinched when she said it made me wonder again if she was Emma. Was she remembering the sensation she'd felt when she'd walked into the room?

"Well, shall we clean up these plates and settle in with our hot chocolate? I'm afraid the power may go out, and we'll lose the hot part of that equation." She chuckled as she rose with her plate.

I scrambled to my feet, leaving Whiskerina sleeping on the pillow.

"I could have taken your plate if you wanted to stay by the fire," Grandmother said.

"Nah, I'm good. Besides, I want extra whipped cream and marshmallows."

"Oh, don't I give enough?"

"You're pretty generous, but I want *tons*."

"I see," she said as she loaded the plates into the sink. "Well, pile on the extras to your heart's content."

"Want me to do the dishes?" I asked.

"They can keep if you'd rather settle in for another installment of the story."

"They won't take long," I said, trying to stretch some time out before the next part. I wanted to ask her about her middle name, but every time I tried to open my mouth to say it, my stomach twisted into a tight knot.

I didn't know why it seemed to be such an issue for me. I just felt silly asking her if she was Emma. I chewed my lower lip as soap bubbles filled the sink, and I rubbed the sponge on the plates to clean them.

"May I ask you something?" my grandmother said, spoiling my chance to make my query.

"Sure," I answered.

"What is it about the music boxes that you find so intriguing?"

I froze, trying to figure out an answer that didn't make me sound crazy. I'd been drawn to both of them, but I'd really been drawn to the mermaid one I'd found in the resale shop.

"Umm, I don't know, I just...I guess I like the songs." I shrugged nonchalantly as I stared at the plate I rinsed.

"I see," my grandmother answered with a bob of her head. "I think that one is rinsed."

"Oh, right," I said, realizing I'd held it under water for way too long. "Sorry, I zoned out for a second."

"Thinking about the music box?"

I shook my head, needing a change of subject. "No, about the story. Velvet Manor. I can't wait to hear more about it and the music box that Emma found there."

My mind went back to the idea that Emma and my grandmother were one and the same. But before I could say anything, Lester shuffled into the room. "Fire's all tended. I'm ready for my dessert."

Grandmother set a plate of cookies on the counter before she crossed back to the slow cooker and ladled the steaming hot chocolate into a large mug.

Lester wrapped his hands around it and sniffed. "Mmm, smells delicious."

He added whipped cream and a few marshmallows as we doled out our portions. I put two heaping spoonfuls of whipped cream on the top of mine and sprinkled the marshmallows on top of that before I stuck a spoon inside of it.

We made our way back to the living room, and I downed two melting marshmallows before we made it.

Only the glow of the fire lit the space now, though we still had power. But I enjoyed the added ambiance as we settled back into our seats.

"Are you all right on the floor? Why not pull a chair over?" Grandmother asked as she uncovered the cookie plate.

"I'm okay. I want to be close to the fire. It's nice and toasty."

My grandmother raised a finger in the air as she rose and left the room.

"Now, you've done it," Lester said with a twinkle in his eye.

"Yeah, must have. Hey, I've been meaning to ask you…" I hesitated, not certain if he'd take kindly to me poking at him with questions.

He sipped his hot chocolate before he answered, "Ask away."

"How long have you been working with my grandmother?"

"Oh, a long time. Even before your grandfather passed away."

"When did he?" I asked. "I don't want to ask in case it's... you know... she's sensitive."

"I think you'll find Althea is a very practical woman. And while she still carries her grief with her in some ways, she's very understanding that people are curious."

I bobbed my head, figuring he'd make me ask her, though I still didn't feel comfortable.

"He passed shortly after your father left for college."

"Oh, that's sad. So, Grandma had an empty nest and then lost her husband."

Lester bobbed his head. "Your father didn't even come home."

"What?" I wrinkled my nose. "Not even for his own dad's funeral?"

"Said he was busy with schoolwork."

I clicked my tongue. "Wow. That was..." I couldn't imagine my parents letting me skip someone's funeral. And what I couldn't figure out was why he and my mom disliked my grandmother so much. She seemed nice.

Our discussion ended when she flitted back into the room, carrying a massive bean bag chair. "I bought this for you. I wasn't certain you'd like it, but why not give it a try now? It must be more comfortable than that old throw pillow."

I leapt from my seat and tossed the pillow back as she set the pink and purple seat near the fire. With Whiskerina in one hand and my hot chocolate in the other, I plopped onto the soft chair.

"How is it?" Grandmother asked as she eased into her seat again.

"I like it. Thank you." I reached for the blanket draped in the cubby of the side table and tugged it over me and my kitty, pulling my legs up under me as I sank further into the beans. "Perfect."

"Good. I'm glad you like it. Now, where were we?"

"They just got to Velvet Manor, and Emma said it was definitely haunted, but that was it. We didn't hear anything about what it looks like outside of the foyer or why she thinks it's haunted."

My grandmother lifted her chin with a grin. "Ah, yes. Well, let's go exploring in Velvet Manor, then, shall we?"

Emma stared at the intricate wood making up the carved railing as she allowed her psychic feelings to settle.

"More than one?" Rose asked.

"I think so. Though I think just one is causing most of the problems. Shall we settle in and do a little exploring?"

"Yes," Rose agreed. "If the foyer is any indication, this place has some real beauty to see."

"I'm going to leave my bag here," Emma answered, shifting it off her shoulder.

Rose grabbed one of the grocery bags from Emma's arms, allowing Emma's luggage to thud to the wooden floorboards. "Good idea. We'll pick it up on our way back through. Let's take these to the kitchen."

They meandered through the halls of the main level to find their way down to the kitchen and pantry. After stowing the groceries, they took a look around the space before climbing back to the main level.

"Want to unpack first or look around?" Emma asked.

"Let's look around," Rose answered. "I'm dying to see more of this place."

"Me too. What I've seen so far has been really beautiful. Let's start at the back of the house and work our way back to our bags."

They toured through several of the rooms, admiring an old library filled with dust-laden books housed on thick wooden built-in shelves. A small sitting room adjacent to it looked out over a side garden.

At the rear of the house, a large ballroom spread out with towering windows that overlooked a blooming flower garden and the surrounding moors, heavy with mists.

"It sure is foggy here," Emma said as she stared at the heavy clouds covering the landscape.

"Yes, it is," Rose agreed. "It may be nice to build a fire and eat by it to keep the chill away."

Emma bobbed her head. "I'll bet it gets cold here at night. Should we move on?"

"Yes, I'm getting hungry, speaking of eating," Rose answered with a chuckle.

"Me too." Emma twisted toward the door, freezing as her features pinched.

"What is it?" Rose asked.

"I could have sworn I saw a figure in the door." Emma crossed to it and peered into the hall. "Hello?"

Only the echo of her voice responded. She shrugged as she wrapped her arms around herself and rubbed. "Must have been a figment of my imagination."

"Or your first encounter with a ghost," Rose answered.

"Perhaps," Emma answered, her brows still furrowed as she stared into the ballroom. "My sense does say something about this room, but I don't know why."

Rose glanced back over the expansive space again. "Time will tell."

"Let's hope so," Emma answered.

Rose rubbed Emma's arm with a consoling smile. "We'll figure it out. We always do."

Emma offered her a nod with a smile that didn't quite reach her eyes before they left the ballroom behind.

They toured a few more rooms, playing a record on an ancient victrola and making a few shots in the billiard room before they made plans to return there after their meal.

"That'll be a fun way to end the night, though I can't make a *shot to save my life,"* Rose said with a chuckle as they picked up their bags to carry them upstairs.

With bedrooms across the hall from one another selected, they settled in, unpacking a few things and swiping away the dust that covered many of the surfaces.

Emma finished and stepped into the hall, slinging the dust rag over her shoulder as Rose emerged from her room. "The only thing with these jobs is the dust."

Rose chuckled at her statement. "Yes. No one ever dusts after the ghosts kick up a fuss."

"I wish the ghosts dusted," Emma answered. "Did you get everything set up?"

"I did. Ready to make some dinner?"

Emma nodded. "More than ready."

"My mouth has been watering for that homemade pizza we planned."

"Me too. I'm excited for the soda with it, too."

"Ah, the simple pleasures," Rose said as they entered the kitchen and started to prepare their meal. "So, you said you think there's more than one spirit here. What gave you that idea?"

"Just a sense, I can't really explain it. But I got the impression there is one dominant one."

"Nefarious or..." Rose spread pizza sauce over the pre-made shell.

Emma's features twisted as she sprinkled cheese over the sauce-covered dough. "I don't think so. It doesn't seem controlling."

"Did the owners give you any information about the haunting?" Rose sprinkled mushrooms on top before she popped the pizza in the preheated oven.

"Nothing outside of a few odds and ends about what had been happening. But I generally don't like to hear their theories. It clouds my judgment I think."

"Hmm," Rose murmured as the timer ticked the minutes away toward their piping hot pizza meal. "Fair enough."

"I did ask them for a history of the house. I have it in my bag. I'll run up and get it and we can peruse it while we eat."

"That sounds good. Do you want to build the fire while you're headed that way? I can deliver the pizza as soon as it's ready."

"Perfect." Emma shot her a thumbs up as she backed from the kitchen. *"See you in a few."*

She hurried through the halls back to her bedroom to retrieve the folder. As she stepped away from her suitcase, the door across the room creaked open a little further.

She froze as she stared into the space near it. Was there a presence lurking there?

A cold draft swept past her, sending a shiver down her spine. *"Hello?"*

No one answered her. She pressed the folder tighter to her chest, waiting another moment before she stepped toward the door.

She shifted it back and forth on its hinges, trying to determine if it had merely fallen further open because of a pitch of the house or some design.

But it stood still at every position she tried. Perhaps the draft had blown it open. Had Rose opened the front door for some reason?

With a deep sigh, she left the room behind and made her way downstairs. The front door remained closed with no sign of Rose in sight.

Emma stepped into the living room and set the folder on a side table before she crossed to the fireplace.

She stuck her hand inside the cold hearth, trying to gauge if the draft could have come from it, but the damper was shut tightly.

After releasing it, she built and lit the fire, poking at the logs until it caught. By the time Rose carried the gooey pizza in, she had it roaring.

They settled into the armchairs nearby and took their first bites, strings of cheese stretching from their mouths to the steaming slice.

Emma wiped her hands on a napkin before she slid the folder closer to her. "Okay, let's see what we can see about Velvet Manor."

"I'm dying to know who built this place. They had a unique taste. Everything is so..."

"Over-the-top?" Emma asked. "It's beautiful, but all the carved woods and the opulent chandeliers. Someone had extremely specific taste."

"Yes," Rose agreed with a nod. "Yet, it has this homey feel."

"I noticed that, too. I wondered if that was more about a spirit here than the decorating, though."

"You think there's a friendly spirit that's making us feel welcomed?"

Emma pinched her eyebrows together as she took another bite of her pizza. "I'm not sure. There's something about this place, though. Gosh, I really wish Mom was here with us."

Rose reached for Emma's hand. "I'm a sorry replacement, I know that."

"You're not," Emma answered. "But she was such a talented psychic. I've been reading her journals, and she is just so... attuned to the spiritual world."

"She had a lot of practice, Emma," Rose said. "Remember that. You'll get there, too."

Emma heaved a sigh. "I hope so. It's just...that's the thing with wishing Mom was here. She could help me get better instead of me figuring it out on my own."

"Yeah, I know. That's what I mean about being a sorry replacement. I can't help, I'm afraid. I don't have any of this psychic sense."

"No, but you do help," Emma answered. "Someone to bounce ideas off of, someone who knew Mom and does remember things about what she experienced."

"Well, I'm happy to do it. And I'm glad I came over for this trip. It's beautiful here despite being haunted."

Emma chuckled at her as the flames in the fireplace flickered and a cold breeze whisked around them. "There's that draft again. And this time I know you didn't open a door."

"Was there one before?"

"Yes. When I was retrieving Mom's journal, my door blew open."

"Or was opened."

Emma nodded. "I'm starting to think it was a curious ghost."

"Well, with any luck, we'll learn more about this curious ghost." Rose set her plate to the side. "Whew, I'm stuffed."

"Me too. And suddenly, I don't feel like reading the history of this place."

"Tomorrow is a new day," Rose answered. "Maybe we should just let the fire die out and head to bed."

"Yeah, the drive took it all out of me," Emma said as she stretched. "Let's wash these dishes, check the fire, and head to bed."

"Sounds good to me."

The collected their things and returned to the kitchen. After finishing their work and checking the fire, they parted ways in the upstairs hall to stretch out in bed.

As Emma lay in the quiet darkness, broken only by the moon's light filtering through the sheer curtains, she stretched her senses, trying to latch on to any entity in the house.

Her eyes slowly closed as she started to drift off to sleep until a noise startled her awake. She shot up to sitting, her eyes wide as she strained to listen.

Tinkling notes floated in the air, a haunting lullaby in the quiet night. Her heart sped as the music continued to play.

Emma clutched the covers tighter around her, goosebumps peppering her skin, as she wondered what the lilting tune would lead her to.

CHAPTER 3

"Was the music from my music box?" I asked as I reached for it on the side table. I twisted the key and let it play. "Was it this song?"

My grandmother lifted her chin. "Now, now...you'll have to wait and see."

"Ugh," I groaned as I let my head fall back between my shoulders. "You always drag it out."

"But you enjoy it." Her eyes twinkled as she stared at me.

"I do," I admitted. "Your stories are so good."

"Thank you. But I'm getting tired after all that driving."

"Like Emma," I said, wondering if she'd latch on to the words and spill anything about who or if she was Emma.

"Yes, just like her. You'll see when you start driving. Lester, I'm going to take Carly to get her learner's permit soon so that she can drive on our next outing."

"Oh, that'll be good. You can switch off and then you won't get so tired."

"My thoughts exactly," my grandmother answered. "Well, shall we clean up and head to bed?"

"Okay, as long as we can have more of the story tomorrow morning."

"Absolutely, but then you'd better get back to your painting before your art tutor arrives later this week.

"I know. I want to get back to it. But as long as I hear the next bit of the story, I'll be tided over until lunch time tomorrow."

"Well, then, we'll hear more over breakfast."

With the plan in place, we washed our mugs and headed to bed. I carried the music box back to my room, setting it on my nightstand before I crawled between the sheets and pulled my fluffy comforter up higher.

The storms continued to rage outside, putting on a light show as Whiskerina curled up next to me, purring softly as I petted her.

My mind played through what it would be like to be Emma in that mansion, trying to search for ghosts.

I reached for the music box and set it playing before I settled back in the pillows, letting my eyes close. My stomach twisted into a knot, almost forcing my eyes open again to scan my room for ghosts.

The music was incredibly haunting, like a sad lullaby that called to me from the past. A cool breeze tickled my skin. With a gasp, I snapped my eyes open, searching the room for a ghost.

I didn't find any, though. I pulled my covers higher, still unsure. With a hard swallow, I reached for Whiskerina to soothe me.

This was silly. I wouldn't know if a ghost was standing right in front of me. I didn't have any psychic talents. I wasn't a psychic witch.

I rolled my eyes at myself. Maybe I was scared because I *couldn't* see ghosts. One could be hovering right in front of me, and I'd never know it.

Of course, all the people in the houses knew it, whether they could see them or not.

Another rumble of thunder and flash of lightning lit my room. I bolted upright and turned my light on, swearing I'd seen a figure in the corner.

I held my breath as I allowed my eyes to adjust to the light only to find an empty corner.

"I really need to stop scaring myself, Whiskerina," I said as I switched off the light and leaned back against my pillow.

With my gaze on the music box, I let the haunting notes wind down and didn't rewind it. I didn't need to hear more of it and keep myself up for the rest of the night.

In the quiet stillness of the room, with the thunder still rumbling in the distance, I finally fell asleep, my dreams filled with images of a Scottish manor.

When I awoke the next morning, dark clouds still hung heavy in the sky. I stared out at them, enjoying the dark morning before I wound my Scottish music box again. In the cold light of day, I no longer thought I saw ghosts running around my room.

Instead, I could enjoy the brooding music while I wondered what Rose and Emma would find in the manor.

When the music died down, I kicked back my covers and slid my feet into my fuzzy cat slippers. I shuffled across the room to retrieve my other music box before I curled under my covers again with Whiskerina.

I studied the outside, filled with nautical symbols before I pressed the locket into the indentation and popped the music box open.

The mermaid inside reached for me, her delicate hand outstretched toward me. I recalled the jolt that shot through me when I touched in in the store. Was that a result of static electricity or was it something else?

My shaky finger reached toward her again, stopping short of making contact. What was I afraid of?

I rolled my eyes at myself as I wound the music box and set it down to play its haunting melody. There was no way I had any sort of "connection" with this object. I wasn't a psychic witch.

These were all just stories my grandmother was telling me. I was acting like they were real.

In all likelihood, some elements of them were real. There probably was an Emma and Rose. And they probably traveled all over the world collecting items like my music box. But they probably didn't eradicate ghosts.

I chuckled at the way it sounded in my head. I pictured them with proton packs strapped to their backs and tan jumpsuits.

I giggled even more, jarring Whiskerina awake at my side. She glared at me before she settled back down for another cat nap.

"Sorry, Whiskers, but I'm starting to think I'm taking these stories way too seriously."

With a deep inhale, I glanced at the mermaid spinning on her platform again. It was ridiculous that I was afraid to touch her because I worried I'd get some sort of cosmic shock.

"Stupid," I murmured to myself.

As she slowed to a stop, reaching out to me once again when the music stopped, I leaned forward and let my finger graze her hand. My heart stopped as another jolt shot through me.

I jerked my hand away, my chest tight. Was it another burst of static electricity?

I carefully set the thing on my nightstand and climbed from my bed. I rubbed my palms against my nightie before I touched her hand again, getting another shock.

I shook my head and kicked my slippers off. My bare feet touched the cold wooden floorboards as I made my way to the light switch and pressed my fingers against the metal screw. Nothing happened.

I crossed back to the mermaid and pressed a finger against her porcelain hand, receiving another shock.

Confusion made my brain fuzzy as I collapsed on my bed. What was happening?

A knock on the door pulled me from my thoughts.

"Carly?" my grandmother called. "Breakfast is ready. Are you awake?"

Heat washed over me. "Yeah!" I shouted. "I'll be right down."

I didn't want her to think I was completely insane. I had to pull myself together. Maybe there was something wrong with the music box. Maybe it generated its own static electricity when it spun or something.

I told myself that's what it was as I rose from my bed, pulled on my clothes, and hurried downstairs.

"There you are," Grandmother said as I plopped onto the stool at the counter.

She slid my fried eggs from the pan onto my plate next to the bacon and toast before she joined me. "I was beginning to worry."

"I was just daydreaming in bed."

"Oh?" she asked as she dipped her bread into her egg yolk. "About?"

"Scotland and Emma and Rose. They weren't…really ghostbusters, right?"

She chuckled at the term. "What do you mean?"

"I mean like…Emma and Rose were real people, right?"

"Yes," she said with a nod.

"And they really went to all of these places, right?"

My grandmother nodded as she sipped her orange juice.

"But...there were no ghosts, right?"

"Well, of course, there were."

My heart stopped as I tried to parse through the statement. "There were?"

"Yes, of course. Emma and Rose were real ghostbusters as you call it."

My forehead creased as she said the words.

"Carly, just because lots of people don't believe it, doesn't mean it's not true."

I chewed my lower lip.

"There's no reason to be frightened."

"I'm not scared, I'm just...confused, I guess."

"About?" she asked.

My heart thudded against my ribs. Should I ask her if she was Emma? Should I ask her about ghosts?

"A lot of stuff, I guess."

"Well, ask away." After a second, she added, "When you're ready, of course."

"Okay, I will. I just...I need to think about what I want to ask."

"How about more of the story in the meantime?"

I grinned at her and nodded. "Yes, I'd like that."

"Good. Well, here we go."

Emma awoke the next morning, the strains of the haunting melody that she'd heard the night before still lingering in her mind. Despite searching, she hadn't found anything that led to the haunting notes.

She shuffled downstairs to the kitchen where Rose was already cooking breakfast. The smell of bacon made her stomach grumble.

"Sorry, rough night," Emma said as she chipped in to butter the toast that popped up from the toaster.

"No problem. Visited by a spirit?"

"Something like that," Emma answered, gliding the knife over the bread.

Rose shot her a questioning glance as she removed bacon from the pan and laid it on a plate. "Really? Anything that will help us with the haunting?"

"Not a thing. It wasn't a ghost, per se," Emma answered. "It was a music box."

Rose finished with the bacon and cracked two eggs into the still sizzling pan, cooking them in the bacon grease. "You found one?"

"Couldn't find a trace of it. But that music just floated on the air for at least twenty minutes."

"Did you identify the room it came from?"

"Seemed to come from everywhere all at once." Emma plopped onto a stool at the counter as the eggs finished frying.

"So, maybe not a music box, but rather a ghost simulating one?" Rose slid the eggs onto a plate and passed one to Emma.

"Maybe."

"You don't think so," Rose said as she sat down next to Emma and grabbed her fork.

"I don't. I think...I think it's really a music box. It sounds like a music box."

"But what music box plays for twenty minutes and seems to come from everywhere all at once?"

Emma stared into space as she bit into her bacon. "I don't know. Maybe I'll hear it again tonight, and you can help me track it down."

"I'd be happy to," Rose answered. "Just wake me up. I'll help you look for it. Maybe we'll even find a lovely music box as a keepsake."

Emma chuckled at the words as she scooped up more of her egg white onto her fork. "Maybe. As long as we help the ghost it belongs to. I don't want to transfer it anywhere."

"Oh, so you read about transference in your mother's journal?"

"I did." Emma wiggled her eyebrows as she grinned at her aunt. *"I'm learning, see?"*

"I knew you would. Transference is a tricky thing, but your mother used it a few times to help spirits. It's not...as frightening as it sounds."

"I didn't find it so much frightening as...sad."

Rose crinkled her brows at the words. *"Sad?"*

"These spirits are so disturbed that they'll latch onto anything to find help."

"Mmm, yes, that's very true. I hadn't thought of it that way. Most people think its nefarious. That they manifest themselves in these objects as a way to leave the place where they are trapped."

"I think it's less about leaving the place they are trapped to haunt others and more about desperately seeking help from someone who can help them. Most people can't."

"You have that part right. Most people have no idea how to assist any of these spirits. In fact, they barely know they are there. They may have the occasional disturbance, but they don't really sense them. Not like you."

"Or you, it sounds like," Emma said. *"You don't seem completely imperceptive like most people."*

"Maybe because I know better."

"Is there a way to enhance your abilities?"

Rose chuckled. *"I don't think I have any abilities to enhance but thank you for the compliment."*

"I do think you have an ability beyond the normal person. Maybe not as much as Mom or me, but I didn't know I had anything until you challenged me."

"Are you going to challenge me?" Rose asked with a chuckle.

Emma shook her head. *"No, but...well, I just wonder if perception can be enhanced. I'm going to do some reading on it. Unless... you prefer I didn't use you as a science experiment."*

Rose grinned at her niece. *"I don't mind at all. I just hope you aren't disappointed in me."*

"Never," Emma said as she polished off her breakfast.

They cleaned up the dishes and explored the house a bit more as the fog lifted from the moors around them.

Emma peered out one of the windows as they passed. "Let's check out the garden."

"Okay," Rose said. "Looks like we may have a stretch of decent weather until this afternoon."

"Yes, I saw the forecast. Rain, rain, and more rain."

"Thunderstorms, too. And you know how ghosts love those."

Emma chuckled at her aunt as they pushed into the crisp Scottish air. "They do seem to be drawn to it. Do you know why?"

Rose lifted a shoulder in response. "Maybe the energy in the air?"

"That could be. I always just thought they put storms in movies to make it scarier. You know, the power goes out. Thunder rumbles, lightning flashes, and bam! There's a ghost."

"Yeah, me too, but I really think you're on to something, there. Maybe the energy from the storm does draw them out."

"Well, I guess we'll test my theory on that today. Perfect weather for it coming in a few hours."

They rounded the corner of the house, making their way toward the back garden when Emma froze. "Oh, good morning."

The man she'd spotted set his shovel aside as he reached down to pull up a clump of weeds and toss them to the side. "Morning."

Emma stepped forward, thrusting her hand out toward. him. "I'm Emma, and this is my aunt, Rose. We're here to– "

"I know why you're here," he interrupted, his tone clipped and short.

"Right," Emma said with a slight smile. "Well, it's a pleasure meeting you. The house and grounds are lovely. You've done a wonderful job."

The man grunted a response to her as he continued to work, his eyes never leaving the ground.

"What did you say your name was?" Rose asked.

"Elias," he answered. "Groundskeeper for Velvet Manor."

"Well, like I said, you've done a lovely job with the place," Emma answered again.

She glanced at Rose, raising her eyebrows.

"Well, we'll let you get back to your work," Rose said.

They stepped past the man, heading for the back gardens.

"You'd be wise to heed the history here."

Both Rose and Emma twisted to face him. "What?"

He finally raised his eyes to theirs. "The history. Mind it. Before you end up a part of it."

CHAPTER 4

My jaw dropped open as I heard the last words. "Was that a threat?"

My grandmother's eyebrows pinched. "No, I don't think he meant it as a threat so much as a warning."

"Mm," I murmured as I wiped the towel over the freshly washed breakfast dish. "It sounded like a threat to me. Hey, speaking of, I have a question."

My grandmother shut off the water and grabbed a towel to dry her hands. "What is it?"

"Did Emma and Rose ever have trouble with the living people? Like they do all this ghostbusting, but did any real people ever give them trouble?"

"Do you mean physically or…because of their talents?"

I shrugged. "Both, I guess. I meant physically. They did all this traveling alone. Wasn't it scary for them?"

"In some ways, I suppose, but in others it was quite invigorating. Were you frightened when we went on our trip?"

I set the dried plate in the cupboard and swung it shut. "No, but…I guess I figured you'd keep me safe."

"Me...an 'old'?" She grinned at me as she used the slang I'd taught her.

"Yeah. Plus, I guess I figured you wouldn't go into any bad parts of town or anything."

"Well, yes, there are precautions to take, but sometimes things happen. You should know how to protect yourself."

"Which is why you're getting me self-defense classes."

"Yes, but not because you should be afraid of the world, Carly, but because you should experience it secure in the knowledge that you can handle yourself if needed."

I chewed my lower lip as I considered it while we walked to my painting studio. "So, did people give them trouble because of their talents?"

"Yes. Some people did. There are those in the world who don't understand it or do not wish to believe it."

"But those people are wrong. I mean, you said these aren't just stories, but they're real. So...those other people are wrong."

"But they don't see it that way," Grandmother answered.

I furrowed my brow as I stood in front of my covered masterpiece.

"Things are not always as black and white as they may seem, Carly. Young people tend to view them as such, but there are so many subtleties. As you grow, you will learn to avoid people who may defame you for things they don't understand."

"I think I'd just avoid people who are rude like that."

"Some of them can be very rude."

I wondered if they were rude to my grandmother because she was Emma.

"I will leave you to your work. We'll talk more this afternoon. And let's plan a trip to town tomorrow to look for that curio."

I grinned at her as I tugged the sheet from my easel. "Okay, that sounds good."

The rest of the morning flew by as I worked on my painting. I'd forgotten how much I had enjoyed creating this image from my own mind. I hoped my teacher would be pleased with my progress when she visited later this week.

After cleaning up my area, I left my painting go in favor of a walk outside for a few minutes before lunch. The sun shined through the trees, dappling my skin with light spots as I leaned against the trunk.

How many people knew about what Emma did, I wondered? And what had people said to her?

I wanted to ask, but I wasn't sure if all my questions were welcome or not.

My grandmother seemed to patiently answer all of them, but maybe I'd become a pain with them.

Plus, the one I really wanted to ask…the one burning a hole through my mind was…did you just know Emma or are you Emma?

I winced at how accusatory it sounded in my mind. If she was Emma, there had to have been a reason that she didn't tell me. Maybe she was afraid I'd be one of those mean people who didn't accept her.

But that couldn't be further from the truth. Although, I did understand it. I was too afraid to tell her I had some connection to the music box I'd bought. I figured she'd laugh at me.

Emma was a psychic witch, but that didn't make me one. She'd probably figure I just had a really vivid imagination and chalk it up to all the stories that she told me.

With a sigh, I pulled myself away from the tree and made my way back into the house.

My grandmother flitted around the kitchen, preparing our lunch. "Did you have a nice walk?"

"Yeah," I answered, trying not to sound as glum as I felt.

"That doesn't sound convincing." She flicked her gaze to me as she flipped a grilled cheese in the pan.

"No, it was nice. I kind of prefer rainy weather, though. But you can't walk around in the rain."

Grandmother chuckled at me as she slid the finished sandwich next to some homemade potato chips. "Where do you want to eat?"

"Can we eat in the living room? I'd like to play more of that game…and of course, hear more of your story."

"Of course," she answered as Lester hurried in, crossing to the sink to wash his hands.

"More of the tale? Have you gotten to the part about the brooding groundskeeper?"

"Over breakfast," Grandmother answered.

"Oh, I always liked that bit. It reminds me of…me." He chuckled as he wiped his hands on a towel and grabbed his plate.

"You're not brooding," I said.

He offered me a pouty stare. "I can be."

I giggled at him. "You're ridiculous. You're so friendly. You wouldn't have threatened anyone."

"I don't think he did, either. He's just…prickly."

We made our way to the living room and settled around the table.

"Carly and I were discussing seeing shades of gray rather than things in black and white this morning."

"Ah, yes. That is wise advice, Althea."

"It's so difficult when we're young, though. Do you remember those days, Lester?" my grandmother asked.

"Oh, barely," he answered with a chuckle. "But what do you mean we? You are still young, Althea."

She chuckled at him. "We are only as old as we feel. And I'm fighting to feel very young. Child-like even. I still enjoy games and fun as much as someone Carly's age. Maybe even more."

"Yes, these young people today are so blase about fun."

"We are not," I argued. "But…fun's just not…fun or something."

Grandmother laughed again. "What does that mean?"

"Like…I don't know…I guess back in your day going to the local sock hop was fun."

"Sock hop?" Now, my grandmother's chuckle turned into a full belly laugh. "Oh, darling, that was well before my time. I've never been to a sock hop. But…it seems to me that you are all more concerned with being cool than having fun."

I thought about it for a second. She was probably right. I was always concerned with if my friends would think my coloring obsession was juvenile, so I hid it from them rather than just doing it because I found it fun. "I guess. There's a lot of pressure, you know? To be what people think you should be."

"Yes, I know. And that's the entire problem with the world. If everyone was allowed to be themselves and excel with their own talents rather than fitting into a cookie-cutter mold, we would all be better for it."

"Now, there you go on your soap box, Althea."

She waved her hands in the air. "I'm sorry. I'll stop. Let's move on to the tale of Velvet Manor."

"Yes," I said with a grin as I bounced in my seat. "By the way…this is fun."

"Good, I'm glad you're learning to enjoy yourself. Now, where was I? Ah, yes…they'd just met the groundskeeper."

Emma glanced over her shoulder as they strolled away from the groundskeeper. "Interesting fellow, huh?"

"Seems like it. I detected a sadness in him, though."

Emma arched an eyebrow at her aunt. "Really? Well, maybe

I'm wasting my time trying to develop your talents with the dead and should focus on the living."

"You didn't get that sense? Something in his eyes."

"No, I thought him a little gruff, but not sad. That's interesting. You may have a talent you don't know about."

"I think it's a talent called age, Emma," Rose insisted with a laugh. "You start to get more in tune with people's feelings as you age."

"No," Emma said with a shake of her head as they strolled through the garden with its early blooms, "don't sell yourself short. That was very insightful."

"And we don't know if any of it is true."

"We may find out," Emma answered, shifting her gaze to the moors in the distance. "It's pretty here."

"Very," Rose said with a nod. "I'm so glad I came."

"Me too. Well, I suppose we should stop wasting our time and head back in to check out the history of this place."

"After we build a fire, of course," Rose said with a shiver. "This damp air isn't sitting too well with me."

"Definitely."

They made their way back into the house and, within minutes, had a blazing fire going in the living room. Emma settled into her armchair next to Rose's and flicked open her folder. "Let's see what we've got."

"Anything interesting that screams haunting?"

"Not really. It seems like pretty standard fair. The family was wealthy. Generations of them lived and died here. But really nothing scandalous or even note-worthy."

Rose heaved a sigh as she curled her legs under her. "Well, I guess we won't nail this one down easily with the history. We'll have to do a little digging."

"Yes," Emma agreed, setting the folder aside as she stared into the crackling fire. "But that's okay. I don't mind poking around this old place one more time."

"I agree. I'm not sure if your mom mentions it in her journal or not, but this has got to be one the best things about her role in solving hauntings. These grand old estates are really beautiful and absolutely fun to explore."

"I'd like to look through the attic. We didn't bother yesterday, but we may find something there."

"Sure. Do you want to head there now or work our way up there?"

Emma let her head rest against the chair as she considered it. "Let's work our way up."

"Yeah, I'd like to revisit that lovely ballroom. It was so beautifully done with that flooring and all the windows."

"And the tapestries hanging on the far wall," Emma said as she rose from her chair. "I'm loathe to leave this fire behind, but let's make our way through the house again before we settle down for our next meal in front of it."

"Sounds perfect to me."

They wandered through the house again, taking their time to comb through each room for any clues about the house's history. When they reached the ballroom, a shiver shot down Emma's spine.

"Ohh," she said as she wrapped her arms around her midriff, "got a chill."

"You need to get back to that fire," Rose answered as she studied one of the hanging tapestries.

"I know. But we have a lot more work to do. We haven't found a thing yet."

"No, we haven't. But we will. Maybe we need to take a nice little break." She bowed at Emma with a grin. "M'lady, may I have this dance?"

Emma chuckled at her as they came together in a formal stance and floated across the floor in a cloud of giggles.

"And now I can say I've danced in a Scottish ballroom," Rose said as they circled around and around.

"Yes," Emma answered.

Rose spun her before she continued to waltz in circles. Emma's eyes turned hazy, her vision blackening at the edges.

"Whoa, can we slow down? I'm getting a little dizzy."

Rose slowed, the smile on her face giving way to concern. "Are you okay?"

Emma's eyebrows knitted as she rubbed her temples. "Uh, I think so. I...don't know. I was getting dizzy."

"Any better now that we stopped moving?"

Emma began to nod before she shook her head. "No. No, it's not. It's worse. It's like I'm still moving in circles."

Rose rubbed her niece's back. "Okay, do you think you can walk? We can go back to the living room and sit down. See if that helps it."

Emma's breathing turned ragged. "I'll try."

"Okay, maybe I should just bring a chair here..."

"No," Emma said. "I'll try to walk. Maybe it'll help."

Rose wrapped her arm around Emma's shoulders, keeping a tight hold of her as she guided her to the door. "Okay, nice and slow."

Emma leaned against her, the room still spinning around her as her vision darkened further. Before they made it to the door, the room turned black. Her knees wobbled, and a worried cry escaped her lips as she slid to the floor and darkness surrounded her.

CHAPTER 5

My jaw flopped open as I stared at my grandmother. "Emma passed out?"

"She did," Grandmother said with a nod. "She never made it out of that ballroom. Something didn't want her to go."

"Something? Like a ghost? How can a ghost make you pass out?"

"Well, some spirits can manipulate things in the world, including humans."

I shifted in my seat, suddenly bothered by the thought. "But ghosts can't hurt us, right?"

"Oh, they can. Spirits must be handled delicately. And nefarious ones can cause all sorts of trouble well beyond the standard mischief we often see in hauntings."

I fidgeted again. "I thought they were just trapped and could be scary but couldn't hurt you."

"They can, although, Emma wasn't harmed. She passed out. That's different."

"But the ghost made her do that."

"Yes, but not to harm her," Grandmother said.

"Then for what reason?"

My grandmother arched an eyebrow. "That is an excellent question. And one we will answer over dinner, perhaps. For now, I think we should go out and enjoy this lovely sunshine."

I wrinkled my nose. "But, Grandma…"

"No buts. You cannot sit around all day listening to me yammer on about these stories."

"But I like them."

"So do I. And we'll share more of it over our next meal. Until then, let's take a walk. We can go to town, select something nice for dinner, maybe."

"Should we go to that restaurant we went to before?"

"There are plenty of others to try. You've barely seen the town." She rose, collecting our plates into a stack. "I guess. Okay, I guess we'll leave poor Emma lying on the ballroom floor." I pushed against the table as I rose from my seat.

She led me into the kitchen while Lester ducked out the door to continue his outside work. "Poor Emma will be just fine lying there until we get back. And I'll show you the antique store I'd like to go to tomorrow."

"Could we go in today?"

My grandmother puckered her lips as she set the dishes in the sink. "Why not? If we don't find anything we like, we'll get in the car and drive to another in the next town over tomorrow."

"Okay," I said with a nod.

We made short work of the few dishes we had from lunch before we stepped into the warm summer day. After a wave to Lester, we continued down the driveway, our feet crunching the gravel.

As we hit the road, the trees shading us from the hot sun, my grandmother breathed out a long sigh. "Ah, isn't this lovely."

"I guess," I said with a shrug. "Mom and Dad would have just driven."

"Nonsense. The town isn't far. And it's quite nice to get some exercise in."

"I don't mind," I said with a shrug. "But I guess it's faster to drive."

She glanced sideways at me. "Are you in a hurry to get there? Have you something vital that must be done?"

"No. I just…I guess people don't like to waste time."

"Ha," she barked out. "People say that. But they waste time continuously. They're always rushing around. But will spend hours scrolling social media. This is not a waste of time. We are exercising, enjoying the day, and talking."

"Yeah, but that's all idle stuff, right?"

"Is it? When did enjoyment become idle? When did we forget to live life rather than simply put our hours in?"

I scrunched my forehead. "I guess I never thought of it like that. Lilac Lane was…really focused on being busy. People's lives were always busy. I just thought that was how you lived life."

"People have forgotten how to live life, Carly. They live it all for show." She waved her hand in the air. "Stop focusing on getting to your destination and start enjoying the journey. Look at these trees. Look at that sky. Smell those wildflowers."

I glanced up at the trees around us before I sucked in a breath. The delicate, sweet scent of flowers filled my nostrils. I'd never taken the time to notice it before.

"I guess it's nice."

"Of course, it is."

I rolled my shoulders back and focused on slowing my steps to enjoy our walk. I found myself smiling at the chirping of the birds and the fluttering of the leaves in the tree as a nice breeze whisked past us.

I also wondered why my father had been so adamant about keeping me away from my grandmother for all these years. She seemed to have a nice outlook on things. But it didn't match my parents' views at all.

They always wanted me to be busy. Be in a sport, try a new hobby, think about college, take another class. And it always was followed up with the point that one of my friends was doing it.

"What about being busy to learn things, though?" I asked, my eyebrows pinching again.

"That's different. But there is no need to be busy simply to be busy. People rush about all over these days, busy, busy, busy, but what have they to show for it?"

"So…it's okay to try a bunch of things?"

"Of course. Try everything. Paint, sing, play an instrument…play all the instruments in the world! Walk, hike, bicycle, skateboard. Play baseball, soccer. Rock climb. Do anything you wish that sounds appealing. But don't do them just to add to your calendar. Do them to explore."

I bobbed my head as the town started to fill in around us.. "Right."

"Explore yourself, Carly. Always. Always challenge yourself. It will keep you young."

"Like you?"

She slid her eyes sideways to me. "I thought I was an old?"

I chuckled. "You are, but like…you're a young old, you know?"

"Well, I suppose that's something. Now, pay attention as we go along. Look at all the restaurants so you can pick the one you want to try."

I tugged my lips back in a grimace as I studied the passing buildings. "Well, which one is good?"

"Most of them."

"Maybe you should pick because you know them all. What if I pick wrong, and we had bad food?"

"Then we'll know not to go there again. Though, I'm quite sure you can find something suitable."

Our conversation quieted as we passed the many shops and restaurants on our path to the antique shop tucked on a side street near the middle of town.

We climbed the front steps and pushed into the shop. A bell tinkled over our heads as cool, dry air surrounded us.

"Hi there," a voice called before the woman stopped, a smile crossing her aging features as she spotted us. "Well, as I live and breathe, Althea."

My grandmother tossed a lock of hair over her shoulder with a smile. "It hasn't been *that* long, Sandy."

"Long enough. We haven't had tea in such a long time."

"We'll need to make a date for it. I've been quite busy. As you may have heard, my granddaughter came to live with me." She placed a hand on my shoulder. "Sandy, please meet Carly."

The woman offered me a smile and a nod. "Pleased to meet you, Carly. And so very sorry for your loss."

I offered her a polite smile, hating when people brought up my parents' death. I know it was natural, but I was still working through the grief and found it awkward. I never knew what to say. "Thanks."

"Carly is still settling in, as can be expected. And we are here in search of a curio or anything that may tickle our fancy."

"Oh, I've got several to choose from. Take a look around and let me know if you have any questions. And do make that tea date before you leave."

"I will. Carly is getting involved in several different things now, so I'll be all alone again."

"Not if I can help it," Sandy answered with a nod that made her blonde bob wiggle.

My grandmother motioned for me to weave my way around the stuffed shop starting with a passage near one of the front windows. It seemed Sandy had quite a variety of things to offer from taxidermy to jewelry to furniture.

As I rounded the corner, I stumbled upon an old Victrola. My jaw unhinged as I stepped closer before shooting a glance at my grandmother. "Look. An old record player. Like the one Emma and Rose heard that story on."

"Yes," she answered. "Very much like it."

"It's pretty neat, huh?"

"Very. Are you interested in old things like that?"

I shrugged as I moved past it. "I just remembered that part of the story. It was cool and creepy at the same time."

My grandmother chuckled as we continued through the shop. I stopped to admire a few crystal cats inside a display case as she moved on to browse down the aisles.

We finished making our way through the shop, finding a few antique curios that could work for my small collection of music boxes. With measurements jotted down and pictures snapped on my phone, we decided to check their fit the following day.

After my grandmother made her tea date with Sandy, we left the shop behind, stepping into the warm sun again. "Well, what restaurant did you pick?"

"I really wish you'd pick it."

"I will not. And there is no reason to be shy. There are no wrong answers."

I shifted my weight, biting into my lower lip. "Well, actually…I saw a burger place on the corner. It smelled really good. But I'm sure you don't want a hamburger for dinner."

"Says who?" She chuckled at me. "I love Smokey's burgers. We'll go there. And we'll also get ice cream for after."

My grin broadened. "Okay."

We walked to the corner burger joint, placed our order, and waited at a picnic table for it to be delivered. With our food in hand, we headed back for home, discussing the curio options along the way.

I had fallen in love with one of the larger ones that had heavy decorative carved scrollwork but wasn't certain it would fit in the spot we'd picked.

As we veered into the driveway, though, my thoughts turned back to Velvet Manor. I forgot all about my curio in favor of learning what happened to poor Emma.

Instead of eating inside, we decided to soak up the remaining rays of sunshine and picnic in the garden.

As the sun started to descend toward the horizon, I took my first bites of the burger, and my grandmother continued her tale.

Emma dropped to the floor, her mind a mix of confusion and terror. The sensation of whirling around continued to make her dizzy. When she opened her eyes again, the ballroom had been transformed. No longer empty and dust-ridden, it gleamed with a fresh shine.

"Aunt Rose?" Emma called, twisting in a circle in search of her aunt.

A dark figure hovered in the doorway. Emma squinted at it. "Aunt Rose?"

The figure moved toward her, a shimmer of blue and white as it entered the room. Instinctively, she backed away a step, but the glowing figure closed the distance before she could effectively retreat.

Her arms rose of their own volition. Warmth rushed through her body as the figure touched her, the sensation of warm flesh against her palms coursing through her.

She twirled across the room, led by her phantom dance partner as music serenaded them from no source she could identify.

"Who are you?" *she asked, desperately searching the formless being for some clue to his identity.*

She received no response as the waltz continued.

"Please, tell me who you are. Are you trapped here? What's happening?"

The spirit continued to whirl her around the dance floor until she became dizzy again. She tried to tug her hands from his grasp, but his fingers tightened around her. "No," *he hissed.*

"Why? Who are you? Please tell me. I want to help."

"Find the portrait," *the voice hissed again.*

"Portrait? Which portrait? Where should I look?"

"Find the portrait," *the ghost repeated.*

They spun faster, sending her dizziness spiraling into a blinding whirlwind that made her stomach flutter.

"Please stop," *she begged, but they continued to spin until her vision began to darken again.*

She tripped over her own feet, falling backward. As she braced to smack into the floor, she squeezed her eyes closed.

She never slammed into anything, though. Instead, a distant voice called to her. "Emma! Emma! Wake up."

Her eyelids fluttered open, and she glanced around the room, her breath catching. "Aunt Rose?"

"Yes, I'm here. You passed out."

Emma pushed herself up to sit, her eyes darting around the room in search of the phantom that had just led her in a waltz. "Where is he?"

"Who?" Rose asked. "Elias? I think he may still be outside– "

"No, no," Emma said with a shake of his head, "I was just in here...with a ghost. We danced. We..."

Rose's features pinched. "No. You've been lying here in my arms since you passed you. You weren't moving."

Emma sucked in a breath, trying to make sense of it all. "But I *saw him. I talked to him. We danced....but the ballroom looked new. He said...find the portrait."*

"Portrait?" Rose asked.

Emma bobbed her head. *"Yes, that's what he said. Find the portrait. I tried to ask questions, but he didn't answer any of them."*

Emma wrapped her arms around her waist before she slid her gaze sideways to Rose. *"Did Mom ever have visions like this?"*

Rose shook her head. *"Not to my knowledge, but...I'm not sure."*

"I'm trying to sort out how seriously we should take this. Was it a figment of my imagination or a vision?"

"I think we should take it seriously and follow up on it, but after we've gotten you some tea and made certain you're okay. I don't want you passing out again."

"Me either," Emma answered with a breathy chuckle. *"And I'm happy to have a warm cup of tea by the fire before we try to track down this portrait."*

Rose nodded as she stood and reached for Emma, tugging her to her feet. With an arm wrapped firmly around her, she led her to the living room, eased her into the armchair, tended to the fire, then rose, dusting her hands. "Now, for the tea."

"I'm not an invalid. I can go make it."

"But you won't. Try to relax there, and I'll be back as soon as I've got the tea made."

"Thank you, Aunt Rose," *Emma answered, tugging a blanket onto her lap.*

She stared at the flames leaping in the fireplace as she waited for the tea, trying to make sense of the vision she'd had. What portrait was the spirit referring to? And how would it help them solve the haunting?

Perhaps it wouldn't. Maybe they were being led into a trap.

The thought sent a shiver down her spine, and she shook involuntarily before she burrowed deeper into the blanket.

Rose arrived a few moments later with a tray. Steaming cups of tea sat on each end, surrounding a plate of cookies.

"Oh, those cookies look wonderful," Emma said with a smile as she grabbed one of the jelly-filled sandwiches and bit into it as Rose slid her teacup and saucer onto the side table next to her.

"Yes, we made a good choice at the shop." Rose settled into her own chair with a sigh. "Well, have you come up with any ideas on this portrait?"

Emma shook her head. "I don't recall any portraits that struck me as we went through the house."

"Looks like it's time to try the attic we've been avoiding."

Emma bit into her cookie with a nod. "Yes. Maybe we'll have some luck there."

"I suppose at least the spirit is reaching out to you. That's usually a good sign."

"Usually," Emma said. "Too bad this one is being so cryptic."

"Just once it would be nice if they told you their story straight out."

The two women chuckled together before they made plans to continue their investigation. After finishing their tea, they spent a few more minutes lounging in the armchairs and enjoying the fire.

"Well, I suppose we should get moving on this," Emma said with a sigh. "I'd like to see if we can make any progress before dinner."

"We may need a picnic lunch in the attic for that."

"Yes," Emma said as she rose and stretched. "It depends on what we find when we get there. Maybe it's empty."

"In a house like this, I doubt that."

"So, do I. Well, let's get a start."

They climbed the stairs to the second story and snaked through the halls to the carved wooden door leading to the attic.

The heavy barrier creaked on its hinges as they swung it open, staring up the steep staircase leading to the space.

"Let's hope we find some answers up here," Emma said.

Rose rubbed her shoulder. "We'll keep searching until we do."

Emma wrung her hands as she continued to stare up into the dark space. "Did Mom ever give up on any of these cases?"

Rose sucked in a breath, her forehead creasing as she searched her memory. "I think she got her ghost every time, but...there were cases where there was nothing happening. And there were those where suicide was an issue."

"Right, those spirits couldn't be helped in a way that we know of, but...did she ever just...not find enough information?"

"I think she usually found it. And we will, too. Don't worry."

"I just feel like...the first three cases we've done had a wealth of information, but this one...there's just nothing."

"Each one is different," Rose said. "Sometimes, your mother spent weeks at a place before she stumbled onto anything substantial. It's not a race."

Emma bobbed her head as she blew out a shaky breath. "Right. Okay, well, let's go see what we can find."

After finding a light switch, they mounted the stairs, approaching the now dimly lit space. Dark, sheet-covered blobs filled it, created a haphazard walkway through the large room.

Emma patted her hands against her thighs as she searched for a suitable starting place. "Well, this looks like it will take a while to sort through. I think we'll be having that picnic after all."

"Yes," Rose said with a laugh. "It's overwhelming."

"It is. Where do you want to start?"

"Pick a corner." Rose shrugged and grinned at her.

"Uh, let's start over there in the far back. We'll work out way across the room and toward the stairs."

"Sounds good."

They picked their way through the objects hidden by draped covers to the back corner, finding a large dresser tucked into it.

"What a beautiful old piece," Emma said as she squatted in front of it to explore the drawers.

"They don't make them like this anymore. Look at the dovetailed joints, and all the intricate rose carvings."

"Yes, the detail is amazing." Emma slid the top drawer shut and moved to the next one down.

She peered inside, sweeping a hand around, but finding it empty. "Too bad the answers aren't hidden in the drawers."

"At least, not so far." Rose pulled open the final drawer on her side. *"Nothing."*

Emma grabbed the pull on the bottom left drawer, giving it a tug, but it wouldn't budge. "This one's stuck."

Rose crinkled her brows, grabbing hold of it and yanking along with Emma. Together, they managed to inch it out slightly. Rose twisted to view the underside to determine if something was holding it shut.

"There's something here," she said, her voice excited.

"What is it? A guide to the ghosts of Velvet Manor?" Emma chuckled at her own joke as Rose worked to free the obstruction.

She finally tugged it loose and raised it into the dim light. "Looks like a journal."

Emma's heart skipped a beat. "A journal? This could give us some of the clues we've been searching for."

She grabbed the leather-bound book from Rose's hands and pulled it open. "Clara Whitmore. Hmm...should we read it?"

Let's give it a try over our lunch and see if we can learn anything.

Emma bobbed her head, climbing to her feet and pulling her aunt up next to her. Would they find the answers they sought in the journal, or would it be another dead-end?

CHAPTER 6

I shivered as a chill swept past me on the night air.
"Oh, they always find stuff in the journals."

"They often do, yes," my grandmother answered, her face barely lit by the pale moon that had risen while she'd told her story.

"So, did this one give them all the answers?"

She offered me a coy smile. "Well, I think that's better told tomorrow. Time for bed now."

"Time for bed? What? I've stayed up way later than this," I cried.

"But we have important business tomorrow, so you'll need your rest."

"I'll survive," I promised.

"I may not," she said with a chuckle. "I don't lament much about aging, but the inability to sleep for two hours and continue on as though nothing has happened is the one thing I regret the most."

I wrinkled my nose. "Really? I feel like there's so much more to regret."

"Such as?"

I shrugged, suddenly not sure what I'd regret about aging. "Like losing your beauty or something."

My grandmother laughed at me. "You don't lose your beauty, Carly, it simply changes. You become beautiful in a different way."

"But people don't like to get wrinkles and stuff."

We picked up our plates and headed back to the house.

"Wrinkles mean you have lived a full life. What are wrinkles, anyway? Laugh lines, crinkles at your eyes from smiling. Would you prefer to have lived a life with no laughter and smiles."

"I guess not." I hadn't thought of it that way. My grandmother viewed what others saw as imperfections as proof that she'd lived. It was a nice outlook.

"Everything changes, Carly. That is the one thing you can depend on. Though, again, I do lament the inability to stay up all night."

"I probably will, too, although I don't do it that often."

"Well, do it now, while you can. When you're my age, you won't be able to without regretting it."

"I'll definitely try it," I said with a laugh as we washed the few dishes we had and bagged the takeout containers for the trash.

"Well, I'll leave you to your decision to stay up or go to sleep. I am doing the latter. Good night, Carly. I'll see you in the morning."

I smiled at her, shifting my weight from one foot to the other before I leaned forward and hugged her. "Good night, Grandma."

She wrapped me in a warm embrace for a moment before she pulled back and smiled. "Good night, Carly."

I climbed the stairs to my room with my kitten in tow and settled on my window seat. Maybe I'd stay up late like my grandmother suggested.

I stared out at the sliver of moon. Dark clouds sailed past it, obscuring it for a few moments.

My mind went to Scotland. I tried to imagine being in Velvet Manor and passing out. Emma lived a frightening life. I wonder if it scared her as much as it scared me.

I shifted on the cushion, letting my gaze slide around the room as a shiver shot through me. "Hello?" I called meekly.

"Well," I said as I stroked Whiskerina's fur, "no one answered me. I guess that's a good sign."

I let my head thud against the woodwork behind me. "Or I'm not a psychic witch so I can't hear them, anyway."

I sucked in a deep breath, my mind returning to the other question looming over me. Was my grandmother Emma?

With no new information outside of my suspicions based on a flimsy piece of evidence, I still hadn't found the courage to ask her.

I practiced a few times in the privacy of my room. "Grandma…are you Emma?"

I shook with my head. "That sounds stupid."

After a moment of gnawing on my lower lip, I tried again. "Grandma…can I ask you something?"

I lowered my voice and tried to mimic her speech pattern. "Certainly, Carly."

"These stories you're telling me. Did they happen to someone else or you?"

My heart thudded against my ribs as I wondered what her answer may be. "What do you think, Whiskerina? Should I ask her that?"

I imagined her throwing her head back and laughing with that full belly laugh she had when she found something really amusing. "No, Carly. I don't talk to ghosts."

Well, at least I'd know. Now, I just had to remember how to say it when I asked her the next day. I promised myself I would as I rose from my seat to change into my nightshirt.

Before I settled in my bed, I wound the music box from Velvet Manor and let it play. The tune sounded like a waltz to me. I wrapped my arms around myself, imagining that this was the music Emma had heard when dancing with the phantom.

I tried to recreate the scene, my mind stretching to remember the steps when my grandmother and I had giggled our way through a dance in the ballroom in Maple Manor.

With my eyes closed, I wondered if I'd feel any ghostly presences, but I didn't.

I wasn't sure I wanted to, really. I opened my eyes, finding my room completely empty outside of Whiskerina. What would I have done if I'd spotted a ghost standing there?

The music wound down, the last few notes tinkling out slowly before it stopped completely. With a sigh, I stared at it, considering rewinding it, but I changed my mind.

Instead, I crossed to the mermaid music box and opened it. I wound it and allowed the haunting melody to fill the room.

Something about it drew me in. I stared at the mermaid, pretending she was a real person. What had happened to her? Why was her song so sad?

Her porcelain hand reached for me, her tiny fingers outstretched. I stared at her crystal blue eyes as my trembling hand closed the gap between us.

My fingers touched cold porcelain, and the shock jolted through me but this time I didn't pull back.

A strange feeling swept through my body, making the airs on my arm stand on end. Dizziness made me woozy, and I blinked a few times trying to dispel it.

It wouldn't go, though, and then things took a turn for the strange. A muffled voice echoed in my mind. I couldn't make out what was being said, but I recognized the warbled voice of a woman.

What was happening to me?

A mix of fear, dread, longing, and loss all roiled inside of me. Before long, though, the fear took over. I yanked my hand away from the mermaid, crying out as I stumbled and slammed to the floor.

Footsteps pounded down the hall and my door burst open. My grandmother stood in her nightgown and robe, her eyes wide. "Carly!"

I scrambled to get up, still feeling a little off. "Ugh, I'm okay."

"What happened?" She hurried over to help me, easing me onto the bed. "Are you hurt?"

"Just my pride," I said with a chuckle as I rubbed the back of my neck."

"Did you trip? Were you lightheaded?"

I shot her a sideways glance, not wanting to admit what had just happened.

"Carly?" She slid a lock of my hair behind my ear. "Has something happened? It's all right, you can tell me."

Could I? What would I say? That I'd been having a strange reaction to a music box?

My eyes flicked to the object before they returned to my grandmother's face.

I wasn't ready to tell her just yet. "I'm okay."

She stared at me for a moment before she bobbed her head. "All right. Well, would you like a cup of hot chocolate before you go to bed? You seem…rattled."

I was, and I very much wanted the comfort of both her company and the hot beverage. "Yeah, that would be great. I, umm, could you sit with me for a little while I drink it?"

"Of course. Maybe I'll even tell you a bit more of the story to get your mind off of whatever may be bothering you."

I cracked a smile at the words. "That would be great, yeah."

"All right." She hesitated before she rose. "And, Carly, if there is something that's bothering you, you can tell me. Whenever you a ready."

I shifted in my seat with a nod. "I'll come with you."

I followed her downstairs to the kitchen and helped with the hot chocolate preparation. We settled in the living room with cookies and warm drinks. I curled into one of the armchairs while my grandmother built a small fire.

As she eased into the chair next to me, I lowered my gaze to the chocolate liquid in my cup, hoping she wouldn't ask about my odd experience again. I still wasn't sure I could explain it without sounding crazy.

"Well, should I tell you the next part of the story?"

I snapped my gaze up with a smile and nodded. "Yes, please."

With another sip of my hot chocolate, I settled back to hear more about Velvet Manor.

Emma set the journal down on the side table, her fingers lingering on the supple leather as she stared down at it. Maybe this would provide them with answers.

"Should we grab our lunch?" Rose asked, pulling her attention away from the book.

"Yes. And then we'll dive into this. I can't wait to see if we can glean any information about what may have happened here."

"Me too," Rose said with a grin. "And I'm hungry."

Emma threaded her arm through Rose's with a chuckle. "So am I."

They made their way to the kitchen, creating a cheese and meat plate and grabbing a few sodas. Emma nibbled on a piece of cheese on their way back up, her mind wrapped up with what they may find in the journal.

They settled into their armchairs, and Emma pulled the book onto her lap. "Okay, let's see what this has to say."

"What tales of Velvet Manor does that little journal hold?"

Emma turned to the first entry, her brows furrowing as she glanced at Rose. "Do you remember who Clara Whitmore was?"

"Uhh, current owner's daughter, right? She died, but I don't know how."

"Hmm," Emma shifted in her seat, "I wonder if it was tragic. Most of these tales have been."

Rose pressed her lips into a thin line. "I know. We may be reading another sad story, I'm afraid."

"Well, let's see how sad and what we can do to help her now if Clara is our ghost."

Emma sucked in a deep breath as she perused the first entry. "Okay, this says she got the journal as a gift for her birthday and is going to document some of her life along with some of her research into the family."

"Oh!" Rose exclaimed. "Goody. Maybe she did some of the work for us."

Emma grinned at her. "Let's hope so. Because we're not doing too well ourselves."

"We're not doing badly, but let's hope this helps."

Emma scanned the next few pages. "Okay, she's documenting her family tree. And she notes that every first daughter has died young."

Rose and Emma exchanged a glance at the words. "Really? Tragically or..."

"She doesn't say, just that when she was gathering dates, she noticed every first daughter died at the age of twenty-three."

"Wow, young."

"Yeah. And she says it doesn't bode very well for her since she's nearly twenty-three."

"Do we know when Clara died?" Rose asked as she built a tiny sandwich out of crackers, cheese, and pepperoni.

"I'm not sure." Emma shifted the book off of her lap and tugged

the folder she'd left on the table closer. "Uhh, Clara died a few months back..."

Heat washed over her as she flicked her gaze to her aunt.

"What?" Rose asked.

"When she was twenty-three."

Rose sucked in a sharp breath, her features pinching. "That almost sounds like..."

Emma swallowed hard. "A curse."

CHAPTER 7

My jaw fell open at the last bit of the story. I set my mug on the side table and shook my head. "No. A curse?"

"Well, that is their working theory. Of course, we'll need to finish the story to determine if they are correct or not."

"But we know they aren't correct, right?"

"How?" My grandmother crinkled her brow.

"Because curses aren't real, right?"

"Oh? Do you know that for certain?" She raised her chin. "Are you an expert in curses?"

I chuckled as I answered. "No. Because curses aren't real."

"Well, we sound certain," she said as she collected our mugs to return them to the kitchen.

I detected the hint of humor in her voice as I followed her. "Should I not be?"

"You'll have to hear the rest of the story, then decide for yourself."

"So, there *is* a curse," I answered with a playful grin as she set the mugs in the sink. "I can wash those."

"We can leave it for morning."

I crinkled my nose. "I'm not that tired yet."

"Oh, I see." She turned on the water before she slid a lock of my hair behind my ear. "Something still troubling you?"

A few things were swirling in my mind, but I felt so stupid saying any of it.

"It's all right, Carly. You can tell me. Whatever it is."

"What if it's something bad?"

She squirted dish soap into the water and let the sink fill. "Bad? What do you mean?"

My mind spiraled more. I hadn't done anything wrong, but what if I had? "I mean...what if I did something bad? Wouldn't you be mad at me?"

She wiped out the first cup with her rag before she rinsed it. "Mad...no. Maybe disappointed or frustrated, but that doesn't mean I don't love you."

I wrinkled my nose, wondering if she'd be disappointed in both my queries.

"Carly," she said as she set the second mug in the drainer and turned off the water, "I don't know much about what your life was like with your parents, but I have a sneaking suspicion it was very different than the life you will lead here. I don't want to see you make mistakes, but sometimes we do. The important thing is that we learn from it. And you must understand, there are consequences to your actions, sometimes they are very, very negative. I won't save you from them, but I will help you learn from them."

I glanced down at the tile floor beneath my feet, my brows crinkling.

"Do you think you've done something bad?"

"I don't know," I answered.

"If you don't know, I can't see how it could be all that bad, then."

I winced, flicking my gaze up to her. "Maybe it's not bad, but...weird. I don't want you to be disappointed in me."

She smiled at me, cupping my chin in her hand. "Carly, the only way I would be disappointed in you is if you thought me that judgmental that you can't be honest with me."

My features pinched. "I don't think that."

"Yet you won't tell me what's on your mind because you think I'll find you weird."

"Okay, fine, but you have to promise not to laugh at me or get mad."

"What a range," she said with a chuckle. "I will neither laugh or get angry. Now, I can't wait."

"Well, there are two things. One you may get mad about, and one you may laugh about."

She grabbed my hand and led me to the living room. We settled in our chairs as the fire dwindled down. "All right, which one do you want to start with? The one where I will be angry or the one where I laugh?"

I forced a laugh, though my stomach tied into a knot. "I'll go with the laughing one."

"All right. I will prepare to stop myself from doubling over in laughter." She grinned at me.

I still felt uncomfortable enough that I didn't find the humor in it. I swallowed the lump building in my throat. "Umm, something weird is happening to me."

Her forehead creased. "Can you describe it?"

"It might take a little bit."

"I'm not going anywhere."

I licked my lips before I plowed into my story. "You know that mermaid music box you bought me?"

"Yes," she answered with a nod.

"Well, you asked me why I liked it…and I didn't really tell you the truth." I paused, searching her face for some sign of what she thought, but she just stared at me, waiting for the story to continue. "I...felt this weird pull to it. Like...something was calling to me."

"I see. And do you still feel it?"

"Yeah," I said, my voice trembling. "And every time I touch it, something happens to me."

"What happens?" she asked, her voice calm and even.

"Umm, like a shock almost. And today I kept pressing my finger against the mermaid's hand, and that's when things got really weird."

She raised her eyebrows in a silent prod for me to continue.

"Uh, it was like I heard a voice or something, but it was all garbled and stuff. And it made me feel really weak."

She pressed her lips together and nodded.

She hadn't laughed at me, but I couldn't read what she was thinking. "Do you think I'm weird."

"Not at all," she answered. "And I am not very surprised to be honest."

I crinkled my brow. "You're not?"

"No. I realized the day you found it. Such a unique piece and tied to a great amount of history."

"Grandma...are you Emma?"

She snapped her gaze to me, studying my face. I wondered if she'd yell at me. But then a grin spread across her features. Maybe this would be the one she laughed at me over.

"I wondered if you'd catch on. You're very bright, so I assumed you would."

"So, you are? All these things happened to you?"

"They did," she answered with a nod. "Yes."

"Why didn't you say anything?"

Her smile faltered a little, and she glanced at her lap. "Well, I...didn't want you to think I was strange when you first came. Your parents sheltered you so much from me.

Our relationship was tentative enough that I did not wish to risk it with what you young people call TMI."

This time, I laughed, my muscles finally loosening a little. "Well, I wouldn't have judged you either. I think it's pretty cool."

"I'm glad you think so. Especially because you are also a psychic witch."

Heat washed over me, and my stomach twisted into a knot. "What?"

My head shook no matter how hard I tried to stop it.

My grandmother huffed out a chuckle as she nodded. "I'm afraid to say you are."

"But...no...no, I can't be. I don't have any powers like Emma...you do. I can't see ghosts or talk to them or get visions."

"But that's not true."

I wrinkled my nose, my head still shaking. "It is. I can't see ghosts. I've even tried to see them, and I can't."

"Oh?" My grandmother arched an eyebrow. "Well, I'm afraid Thornwood Estate is severely lacking in ghosts of late, so you might not have much luck."

Was she mocking me? I glance down at my lap as I tried to decide.

"Oh, I don't mean to poke fun, Carly, but...if you've tried here...I assure you, the spirits have been dismissed."

"But how do you know I can see them, then?"

"Because you are seeing them. Your reaction to the music box from the shop proves it."

My features remained pinched as I shook my head once again. "But...no...I don't like *see* a lady or anything."

"Of course not. You need trained and guided. But you are making contact. You just don't know what to make of it right now."

My jaw remained unhinged as I tried to process it all.

"Carly, you are no different than I was at your age. Approaching your eighteenth birthday in just a few weeks is causing all sorts of things to happen within you. And it will not be easy, but I assure you that you have psychic powers."

I slumped back in my chair, my chest tight as I tried to understand what had just happened. All my questions had been answered. My grandmother was Emma. She had been the one setting all the spirits free in all of these houses. And I apparently had the same powers she did.

I couldn't wrap my head around it. A variety of emotions raced through me ranging from fear to excitement.

"It is quite a bit to take in, Carly," my grandmother said, her voice soft.

"No kidding," I answered, my voice breathy.

"You need time to process it."

"I don't know if I can. I feel like I'll never get used to it."

She chuckled. "Oh, I thought the same thing, but it's amazing how quickly you'll get used to it."

I offered a nervous chuckle. "I don't know about that."

"Well, we'll start you slowly," my grandmother said, snapping her gaze to me, "unless you prefer not to."

I hadn't expected to be asked that question. "Do I have a choice?"

"Of course. You can ignore your powers or hide them."

I shifted on the cushion, still unsure. "I didn't think I had a choice. I...I don't know."

"And that's okay," my grandmother said. "There's no need to decide anything tonight."

I glanced at her, trying to read her face. "You'd be disappointed in me if I didn't use them, right?"

She offered me a fleeting smile with a shrug. "Well, of course, I would love to see you use them, but it's a personal choice. And it's not for everyone."

"But you did it."

"I did, yes. As did my mother and grandmother."

I crinkled my brow. "Wait, did my dad…"

"No, darling. Men in the family do not have the gift. Only women. So, it skipped a generation."

I nodded. "That makes sense."

It also made sense on why my parents didn't want me anywhere around my grandmother. They were afraid she'd tell me how different I was. They didn't want me to be different.

"Your father didn't understand." My grandmother glanced wistfully at the dying embers in the fireplace.

My heart went out to her. My father had rejected her and kept me away from her just because she was different, and he didn't understand it. It was probably why she'd changed the names of the people in her stories. She was worried I'd do the same.

"I'm not sure I understand yet, but I'd like to," I answered. "I'd like to at least give it a try."

Her features brightened a little as she glanced at me. "All right. We'll do that, then. As I said, we'll start small."

"Okay," I answered. "That sounds good. I don't know how I'm going to do with this."

"Oh, I'd say quite well. You've already begun exploring it on your own, which is excellent. With some guidance, I'd say you could become quite powerful."

"Do you think I'll be able to help the spirits like you?"

"Yes, I think so. They're already reaching out for help. And you have quite a strong sense of it. You noticed that music box. Someone is looking for help. A spirit is attached to it."

The words sent a shiver down my spine, and I shuddered.

"Don't worry, I don't believe she will harm you or I wouldn't have allowed you to keep it in your bedroom. But she will reach out, I believe."

"But not unless I touch the mermaid's hand, right?"

"Not necessarily. As you attune to her, she may reach out more in dreams and even manifestations."

"Will they be scary?" I asked.

"They may be. Which is why I'm glad you told me about your experience. Now, I can guide you. There is no reason to be frightened, but your first few experiences may make your hair stand on end."

I winced. "Wow. I don't know if I'll be able to sleep ever again."

My grandmother chuckled. "Oh, it's not all that bad. And you know what is coming, so you can be prepared."

"Right." I sucked in a deep breath, still wondering how all of this was going to progress. Would I ever get to a point where I was as calm as my grandmother? Would a teen ever sit across from me listening to stories about how I'd dispatched ghosts?

"I promise you, Carly, you'll be fine. I will make sure of it."

I smiled at her, glad to have her on my side.

"Now, do you think you can sleep, or would you like a bit more of the story?"

My smile broadened, and I clapped my hands together. "Story!"

My grandmother chuckled and nodded. "All right. Emma and…" She chuckled, glancing down at her lap. "Well, I guess I don't need to say Emma anymore, do I?"

"Not unless you want to," I told her.

She shook her head. "I think I'll stick to the truth."

I nodded at her as she launched into her story.

I shifted in my seat as I glanced at my Aunt Rose, a cold heat washing over me. A curse could change everything.

"Let's not jump to any conclusions," my aunt said. "We don't know it's a curse. But it sure sounds like one."

"Let's keep reading." I pulled the book open again and turned to the next page. "Clara is detailing more of her research into the family. She notes all the deaths of the first-born children were from illness. The girls would fall suddenly ill months before their twenty-third birthday, then die within a week of turning twenty-three."

"Okay, this is sound more and more like a curse."

"Or really bad luck," I answered. I scanned a few more pages but didn't find anything mentioned about a curse. "Clara hasn't found anything about any curses."

"She may not have dug far enough. Is there any lead up to her death?"

I turned the page and sucked in a deep breath. "Sadly, I think there is."

"Well, read it aloud," Aunt Rose answered with a sigh. "We'll get through it together."

I offered her a tight-lipped smile as I read the next entry. "'I've been working through the family tree and noticed that the deaths of the daughters started in the late seventeen hundreds. It's consistent for centuries. Which makes me nervous since I'm going to turn twenty-three soon. I hope this is just a weird coincidence.'"

With a flick of the page, I kept reading. "In the next entry, she says she's going to search the house for journals to see if she can learn anything about the deaths from them. But she got sidetracked from the task because she had a headache that made her dizzy."

"Uh-oh," Aunt Rose said with a wrinkle of her nose.

My stomach had already twisted into a knot. Hindsight being twenty-twenty, I assumed this was the start of what would be the illness that killed her. "Yes, I thought the exact same thing."

The next journal entry detailed a few days being spent in bed with the vertigo and a sick stomach. "'I hope to be back to my research soon, though.'" Tears filled my eyes as I spotted the smiley face at the end.

"After this," I continued, "she seemed to recover. She mentions... oh..." A grin came over my face, and I shot my aunt a knowing glance. *"She's met Elias. And she thinks he's very handsome."*

"Aw, do we have a budding romance?"

I smiled to myself as I nodded. "I think so."

With a flick of the page, I read on, detailing Elias giving her a bloom from the garden, a date at the local pub, and a kiss shared under the moon.

"That's so sweet," Aunt Rose said. "Young love."

I grinned at her with a nod before the smile slid from my face. "But..."

Aunt Rose matched my expression, her shoulders slumping. "She dies."

"I wonder if that's why Elias is so...gruff," I said. "It sounds like they were very much in love."

"Losing someone will do that," Aunt Rose answered.

With a sigh, I read on, bracing myself for tragedy. It came sooner than I expected. Clara detailed canceling an evening out with Elias after another blinding headache. "She says," I read, "the dizziness was so bad, she couldn't stand up, and there was no way she could go to the fair with him. She spent the night in bed. When she wasn't better by the next morning, she called her mother in London for advice."

"What did she say?"

"She told her to see the local doctor."

"And did she?"

I sucked in a breath and bobbed my head. "Yes. She spent the morning debating it, but then called when she'd barely had any relief. The doctor made a house call, due to her dizziness."

I flipped the page to read on. "He thought she was suffering from an ear infection and gave her antibiotics to clear it up. A ten-day regime with a follow-up visit at the end."

"How does that go?"

I winced as I turned the page, spotting the next entry dated three days later. "*She's not doing any better. She's considering calling the doctor back, but she's going to give it another few days.*"

Aunt Rose clicked her tongue. "It's like watching a horror movie, and you want to shout, 'Don't go in there!'"

"I know," I said, my heart sinking as I continued to read a story that I knew would end in tragedy. "She's so sick, and no one knows it."

We read on as Clara took another turn for the worse. Elias, who stuck by her side, tending to her, called the doctor again.

"*She says the doctor recommends her going to Edinburgh to see a specialist.*"

I turned the page to read the tragic news. "*Elias took her to the specialist, the news is not good.*"

I smoothed the tear-stained pages as tears formed in my own eyes. "*She's been diagnosed with a rare form of undetectable cancer. She's only been given a few weeks to live.*"

"Oh, no," Aunt Rose said with a shake of her head.

I wiped a tear from my cheek. "Well, we knew it was coming, didn't we?"

"Still doesn't make it any easier," Aunt Rose said as she reached for my hand.

With our fingers intertwined, I read on, my jaw dropping. I flicked a shocked gaze to her. "*Elias and Clara got married in a secret wedding before she died.*"

"Really?" Aunt Rose asked. "Wow. That's...no wonder he's so heartbroken."

I turned to a new page, finding only one word scrawled across it in shaky handwriting. The remainder of the pages were blank. "There's only one word after the final entry talking about their secret marriage."

"What is it?"

"Portrait," I answered.

Aunt Rose shifted in her seat, a finger rubbing her lips. "I wonder if Elias knows anything about that."

"I'm almost afraid to ask him. This is fairly recent. I'm certain he's still grieving."

"I'm sure. He is, too, but...I think we need to know if we're going to help."

With a deep sigh, I set the journal aside and stood. *"Let's see if we can find him."*

We left our cozy chairs behind and stepped back into the crisp Scottish air in search of the brooding groundskeeper. A first pass through the garden turned up nothing.

"Maybe he left for the day," I suggested.

Aunt Rose pointed to a small car tucked in a corner near a towering tree. *"I'd bet that's his. I saw a toolshed earlier. Maybe there."*

I followed her through the garden to the edge of the property, finding a small shed hidden by a large row of bushes. My heart pounded hard as I pushed the creaky door open and peered in, finding Elias cleaning a set of hedge trimmers.

"Hello, again," I said with a tentative smile.

"Need something?"

"Information," I said with a wince as Aunt Rose stepped into the small space next to me.

He turned back toward the trimmers. *"Can't help you."*

"Can't or won't?" I asked.

"We read Clara's journal, Elias," Aunt Rose said, her voice firmer than mine, *"we know about the secret wedding."*

He snapped his gaze to us, his features pinched. *"Don't you go making no trouble now."*

"We don't want to. We just want to help. In her journal, Clara mentions a curse. We're trying to get to the bottom of it to help the spirits trapped here, but...we need more information to do that," I said, my voice pleading.

He grunted, shaking his head. *"Yeah, she thought there was a curse. But it killed her before she could figure it out."*

His features twisted as tears filled his eyes. "She spent those last days rambling nonsense. My poor Clara."

"Nonsense?" I prodded. "I'm sorry, but...maybe it wasn't nonsense. She may have had more clarity in her final days when it came to what was happening in the house."

He twisted to face us, his cheeks tear-stained. "She just kept saying I had to find the portrait. I had to stop the curse."

"Portrait?" I questioned.

He nodded. "Find the portrait, before everyone dies."

CHAPTER 8

"So, is the portrait cursed?" I asked after a wide yawn.

My grandmother rose from her seat. "That, Carly, is going to have to wait until tomorrow. I'm tired."

"I am, too, finally. I guess hearing about your stories helped relax me."

"Good. Hopefully, you can get some sleep, then. I'll see you in the morning."

I climbed from my seat with a nod. "See you in the morning, Grandma."

We climbed the stairs and exchanged a hug outside my door before I slipped inside. Whiskerina lay in the middle of my bed, sprawled out. She's grown so much since I got her, she now took up too much space when she stretched.

I shoved her over a little, earning a glare from her.

"Sorry. You shouldn't have taken over the entire bed," I said to her.

She flicked a paw in the air at me before she rolled onto her other side. As I stroked her fur, settling back into my pillows, I wondered if my grandma had let me get a cat because I was a witch.

I grinned at the statement, laughing a little in the dark room. "Do witches really have cats all the time, Whiskerina?"

I didn't expect her to answer me even if I was a witch, but it made me wonder if the stories were true. Was Whiskerina a familiar?

With a shake of my head, I dismissed the ridiculous idea. I was still working to wrap my head around what had just transpired. My grandma was a psychic witch who helped all sorts of spirits from being stuck here.

She'd traveled the entire world, freeing them and saving them.

And I was going to follow in her footsteps.

The prospect excited me, though I felt nervous, too. What if I was no good at it? My grandmother had figured it out all on her own. I never would have been able to do that.

She'd said otherwise, telling me that my sensitivity to the music box had meant I showed promise and would likely have discovered my talent on my own, but I didn't think so.

And despite her promise to guide me, I couldn't help but think I'd never measure up to what she'd done in her life. After all, she'd lost her mother before she knew anything about her talent and still managed to figure it all out.

My forehead pinched as I realized my grandmother had been orphaned at a young age, too, just like me.

She'd never known her father, and her mother had been killed while trying to help the spirits.

It made me feel closer to her, like we were kindred spirits.

As I flopped on my back, I vowed to work hard so she'd be proud of me. She had been so kind and accepting when I'd come here, and now we shared something truly special.

The thought warmed me as I drifted off to sleep.

I awoke late the next morning. Peeks of the mid-morning

sun poked in and out of the clouds as I rose and stretched before heading downstairs with Whiskerina for breakfast.

"There you are," Grandmother said as I popped into the kitchen.

"Sorry, I didn't mean to sleep this late."

"It's fine. I slept in, too. And you're young. You're supposed to sleep late."

She slid two pieces of French toast from a pan onto a plate and set it at my spot on the counter.

I sank into the seat after dumping a can of wet cat food into a bowl and setting it in front of Whiskerina.

"Grandma," I said as I cut into the fried bread, "did you get me a cat because witches have cats."

She burst into laughter before taking a sip of her morning tea. "Ah, you've caught me."

My features went slack. "Seriously?"

"Well, every good witch has their animal companion. And cats tend to be a favorite because of their savvy instincts."

"I thought that was like all fiction."

My grandmother grinned at me. "Some fact, some fiction. Cats have excellent instincts, especially around spirits. Whiskerina can help keep you safe as a young psychic. I wanted you to have bonded with her before you began your journey."

I licked my lips, trying to make sense of it all as Lester pushed through the back door and wandered into the kitchen. "Another set of storms blowing in this afternoon. I wanted to see if you wanted me to run to town for any provisions. These ones are doozies, looks like. We may be in for the next day or so."

"Oh, maybe we should stock up a little. Comfort foods, in particular. Cozy things to eat by the fire."

"Cheese," he said with a grin.

"Plenty of cheese," she answered. "We'll make a charcuterie board for this afternoon, and while the storm rages on, we'll learn about the portrait."

"Oh, so you've gotten to the portrait, have you? Now, that's one of my favorite parts."

I narrowed my eyes, wondering if Lester was aware that the stories were about my grandmother. Last night, she'd told the story from her perspective, but would she use Emma's name again when Lester was with us?

"Yes. We've just gotten to it. So, you'll get to hear all about it this afternoon. Oh, and in other news, my clever granddaughter has figured this all out."

Lester's eyebrows shot up, and he shifted his gaze to me. "So, you realized who Emma was, did you?"

I smiled as I poked a fork at my grandmother. He bobbed his head. "I've been waiting for you to realize. Makes it more fun, don't you think?"

"And scary. I can't believe some of the stuff she's done at barely older than my age."

"Well, it was a different world back then, too," Grandmother said. "But you'll do them, too. In fact, I've already received several requests from people for your help."

I shifted on my stool, my stomach twisting. What if I wasn't any good at this?

"Don't worry," my grandmother said as she stroked my hair, "you won't take anything on until you're ready. We'll start with that music box you're already drawn to, to build your skills."

I sucked in a deep breath and nodded. "Okay, good."

"But not today," she said, holding a finger in the air. "You have your art to work on this morning."

"And then we'll shut ourselves in from the storm and listen to more tales from the Scottish countryside," Lester said with a grin. "Carly, anything special you want from the store?"

"Ice cream," I said with a smile. "We can have it after the cheese."

My grandmother offered Lester a coy grin. "You heard the girl. Ice cream it is."

"And all the fixings," Lester added. "All right. I'll head into town."

"And I'll go work on my painting," I answered as I rose with my plate in hand.

After washing and drying it, I headed for the studio to work on adding detail to the room I'd imagined in my head. The work was slow-going. My mind couldn't seem to focus, wondering how things would play out with me and the music box.

I wanted to get started, to see if I'd be any good at it, but I also worried I'd be terrible.

Before long, the skies started to darken, plunging the studio from its warm natural light to a dark space. I set aside my tools for the day and left my painting behind, heading for the kitchen.

I found my grandmother creating our lunch tray, and Lester stealing bits of cheese as she cut them.

"Hey, I don't think you're supposed to be eating that yet, it's not lunchtime," I teased.

"Almost," he answered. "And the storm is starting. We were supposed to eat the cheese during the storm."

"We were supposed to eat it for lunch in front of a roaring fire while the rain pelted the windows and banged on the roof, and the thunder rumbled overhead."

"Oh, my," my grandmother said with a grin. "That was quite a lovely description. Have you thought about writing?"

"No," I said with a chuckle. "I'm just dramatic."

"Drama is the point of books," she answered. "We'll explore it more with your education once you decide which route you'll take."

She cut up another block of cheese and laid it out on the tray as I fished crackers from the cupboard, eager to settle down and hear about this portrait.

Before long, we were tucked in the living room with our feast as the thunder rumbled overhead. Lightning tore through the sky every few seconds as the storm bore down on us.

"This is the perfect setting for this part of the story," Lester teased.

A shiver snaked down my spine as the thunder boomed again and rain pounded the roof over our heads.

My grandmother bit into a piece of cheese, a coy expression on her features as she began to tell her story.

Aunt Rose and I glanced at each other at the words. "Portrait?" I questioned. "Have you any idea what she meant by that?"

"None," he answered. "But she was..."

Tears glistened in his eyes as he spoke of her. "She was...so sick. Delusional, I think."

I laid a hand on his arm, a meager consolation for his pain. "I don't believe she was. I think she was killed by a curse. And I think she knew at the end that she would need help in the afterlife."

He glanced at me, a tear falling to his cheek. "You think she... she's...still here?"

"I'm not sure, but I sense several spirits in the house."

"She's not doing the things they say." He curled his fingers into a fist and slammed a hand on the table.

"No, I don't believe she's causing any dangerous disturbances, but that doesn't mean she's not still here."

"What do you mean, then?" he asked.

I glanced at my Aunt Rose who offered me an encouraging nod. "I mean...she may be trapped by a nefarious spirit. The nefarious one is the one doing the dangerous things. Often, they feed off of other souls they trap here."

"Feed off of them?" His voice took on an incredulous tone as he grimaced. "My Clara...she's fodder for some...evil spirit?"

"We don't know the extent of what is happening," Aunt Rose said. "But we'd like to find out. If there's any information you can offer on the portrait or anything she may have mentioned during her research or...even near her death."

He shook his head, his features pinching. "No, I just...I know it was none of the portraits hanging in the house. She never mentioned a specific one. Just kept saying to find the portrait. So... it must be hidden."

I nodded my head, agreeing with the detail. "Yes, it must be stored somewhere in the house. We need to find it."

Aunt Rose bobbed her head in agreement.

"Thank you, Elias, for the information. We'll start a search for this portrait."

"I'm happy to help," he answered, rising from his stool. "I know the house pretty well."

I smiled at him. "We'd love your help with the task. It may even help for you to be in the house. It may strengthen Clara's spirit, and she may be able to guide us."

He shifted his weight, uncomfortable with the idea, but still willing to press on. "Going to be a bad storm here this afternoon. You ladies have enough provisions for the three of us? I can run into town and pick up a few things before it blows in."

"If you wouldn't mind, it may be best if we stock up," Aunt Rose said. "Then we'll begin our search."

"Of course. I'll pick up some essentials and meet you back here."

We parted ways, with Elias leaving his work behind in favor of a quick shopping trip while Aunt Rose and I made a few preparations for our evening meal while vetting ideas for the location of the portrait.

"You know, we never really dug into all the stuff in the attic," Aunt Rose suggested. "Maybe we should start there."

"I agree. It's a likely spot for the portrait."

We finished with our preparations just as Elias returned with the haul of groceries. As we settled with our meal, the thunder roared outside, causing the lights to flicker a few times.

"Is there a generator?" Aunt Rose asked as her eyes went up to the chandelier overhead.

"Aye," Elias answered. "Out here, you need it. Only runs portions of the house, though. A lot of it will be dark."

"That's okay," I answered. "We'll use flashlights or lanterns for our search. I think it's important that we find this portrait sooner rather than later."

Elias eyed me for a second over his soup bowl. "Do you...feel anything?"

I set my spoon down, my eyebrows pinching.

"You said maybe my presence could help. Do you feel anything? Anything from Clara?"

"Unfortunately, nothing significant has changed, but that doesn't mean your presence isn't helping. It just could be imperceptible to me unless we're in a specific part of the house."

"That's an interesting statement," Aunt Rose chimed in. "I wonder if visiting Clara's bedroom would be a good place to start. If Elias's presence is strengthening her, she may reach out."

I nodded. "She could give us a clue about this portrait."

Elias shifted in his seat, his chin lowered almost to his chest.

"Elias?" I asked. "Is that all right with you?"

"I haven't...I haven't been in her bedroom since she died. I'm not sure I can go back in there."

I reached across the table to pat his hand. "We don't have to do it if you don't want to."

"I want to help," he answered. "I just...I'll apologize ahead of time if I break down."

"No one will blame you for that," Aunt Rose assured him. "It was a very difficult thing that you went through. And if you'd like to go inside alone first, we can certainly wait outside."

ENIGMATIC ECHOES

He slid his spoon around the bowl a few times before he raised his eyes. "Can we try to search for the portrait first? Maybe go inside after if we have no luck?"

I offered him a tight-lipped smile. "Of course. There's no reason to rush things. In fact, if you aren't ready to go inside her room, it could hurt instead of help."

"I don't want Clara to hurt anymore." Tears shined in his eyes as he said the words.

I nodded at him. "We'll tackle the attic. There's plenty to look through up there."

"Yes," Aunt Rose agreed. "It could take us the rest of this evening and part of tomorrow."

We finished our meal, changing the subject to a lighter topic, and, after cleaning up the dishes, climbed the stairs to the attic.

"Shall we start in that corner?" I asked the others, pointing back to it.

Elias shined the flashlight into the dark space, his features ashen.

"That's where we found Clara's journal," I said.

"Aye," he answered after a moment, "that was her dresser. She must have put it there the day I found her out of her bed."

He shook his head, his features pinching. "She was so weak, I had to carry her back."

I pressed a consoling hand against his shoulder, understanding his raw pain. My mother's death was still fresh for me, and it had been over a year.

"Well, we can work over there if you'd like to take another corner," Aunt Rose suggested.

"Aye," he said with a nod, "I'll start over here."

With our agreed upon workspaces sorted, we each headed for our start location. After only a few minutes of searching, thunder boomed again and the attic plunged into darkness, lit only by the flashing of lightning outside the small oval windows.

Flashlights and lanterns flickered to life, lighting up the space and casting long shadows across it. A shiver snaked down my spine as we uncovered several paintings, none of which were the portrait we sought.

"I wonder how we'll know it when we see it," Aunt Rose asked. "There are several portraits in the house, and we know it's not those. But there could be several in storage, too."

"I'm not certain, but I hope we will."

She nodded as we continued our search. We combed through the attic's offerings until the wee hours of the morning, finding nothing but dust and cobwebs amongst the stored items.

With a shake of my head, I leaned against a support beam and swiped at the sweat beading on my brow after the work of shifting a large dresser aside only to discover nothing behind it.

"Well, I suppose we should move it back," I said as Aunt Rose rested on the floor, her head drooping between her arms.

"Ugh, give me a minute."

"You ladies rest, I'll handle it," Elias said.

"No, no," I answered, "I'll help you."

As I pushed against the pole to straighten, something shifted. I whipped around to face the beam, my eyes narrowing in the dim light to study it.

Aunt Rose gasped. "Althea, look!"

I spun toward her, then followed the line of her gaze. In the paneled wall we'd just uncovered, a hole now gaped. "It must have been triggered by the mechanism I touched on the beam."

Elias shined his flashlight into it, discovering a rectangular item draped with a cloth.

My heart skipped a beat as I approached, exchanging a glance with him. "Do you think..."

"One way to find out," he answered. He handed off his flashlight to me and crawled into the passage, wrangling the item free.

Aunt Rose stood, closing the distance between us. Elias finally managed to free the thing, emerging from the passage and balancing it against the corner of the dresser.

With a lick of his lips, he glanced at us. "You ready?"

I nodded, and he tugged the sheet away from the object.

A gasp escaped me, and my hand flew to my lips to cover my gaping mouth. I wrinkled my nose as an overwhelming nausea washed over me, and my hairs stood on end. "This is the portrait. This is it."

"How do you know?" Aunt Rose asked.

"Because," I answered, "it's evil."

CHAPTER 9

𝓘 dropped my plate as the thunder boomed and lightning tore through the sky at just the moment that my grandmother said the fateful words. It clattered across the area rug with a muffled thud.

I tugged my lips back in a wince as I tried to reach for it from my bean bag chair. "Oops, sorry."

"Someone took that twist hard," Lester said with a grin, his teeth gleaming in the warm firelight.

"Well, yeah," I said with a chuckle. "She said the portrait was evil."

Lester shifted in his seat, his eyebrows flicking up. "Frightening, isn't it? Sometimes, I don't know how Althea faced what she faced, and at such a young age."

"Me either," I answered. "I'm scared just sitting here. I can't imagine looking at an evil painting. But…how did you know it was evil, Grandma?"

"Well, that's another part of the story, but we should clean up after our meal before we settled in for that."

I let my head fall back between my shoulder blades. "You always stop at the worst times."

"But it keeps you on the hook, doesn't it?" She winked at me.

"Uh, yeah," I said with a chuckle. "It does because you always leave me on a cliffhanger."

"Yes, I do. Now, do you want to settle with some dessert and hear a bit more?" My grandmother asked as she retrieved my plate from the area rug.

"I'll do the dishes," I promised as I climbed from my chair.

Both my grandmother and Lester chuckled at my enthusiasm.

"You better keep those tales coming, Althea. You'll have a built-in dishwasher."

"Oh, I have plenty of them," my grandmother answered as we made our way to the kitchen.

I turned on the water and let it warm up while I squirted soap into the sink. "So, how many spirits have you freed, Grandma?"

"Oh, I couldn't count them now. You know, I used to think I'd keep this running count in my head, but I lost track. I do remember, though, each and every story."

"In detail," Lester said, dishtowel in his hand as he awaited the first washed dish.

I filled the sink and started my chore as my grandmother filled bowls with ice cream and all the fixings. "Carly, hot fudge or caramel?"

"Both," I answered.

"Both!" she exclaimed. "All right. Both it is."

I finished with the last dish and handed it off to Lester. "Do you think one day, I'll have all these stories to tell?"

My grandmother finished with the ice cream bowls, licking the spoon before she slid it into the soapy water. "I have no doubt. I think you'll make an excellent psychic, Carly."

My stomach twisted into a knot as I got excited and anxious at the same time.

"Now," my grandmother said, wagging a finger in the air, "that does not mean that you're going to solve things immediately or be able to dispatch spirits with ease without some practice."

"I feel like you didn't have any practice," I said, cupping my bowl in my hand as we shuffled back to the living room to settle into our seats.

"Oh, I had plenty. And I had Aunt Rose's help along with my mother's journals."

I licked some of the caramel off of my spoon before I wobbled it toward her. "Do you still have those?"

"My mother's journals?"

I bobbed me head, the sweet fudge and caramel tickling my taste buds.

"I do. I'll always treasure them."

I stared down at the scoops of ice cream in my bowl. "Do you think I could read them?"

Her features brightened. "I would love for you to read them. I'm so pleased you're interested."

"Well, it sounds like she was a wealth of information. And while I'm practicing, I thought it may help me."

My grandmother licked the back of her spoon with a nod. "Oh, they will. I'll get them for you tomorrow, and you can read them at your leisure."

I grinned at her. "Thanks. And…can we start to practice tomorrow? With music box?"

"Of course. But…we won't rush. You also have your painting lesson."

"And we need to plan our next road trip. It's going to be so much more fun knowing that you were the one going to all of these places."

My grandmother grinned at me, her excitement obvious.

"It will be quite fun. Lester, would you like to join us on any trips?"

"Oh, maybe a few here and there. I've never seen most of the places you've traveled."

"Good, then Carly and I will make a plan, and you can join in when you'd like." My grandmother nodded at him.

For the first time in a long time, I felt like I had a real family. Funny, you'd think I would have felt that with my own parents, but I never did. Our lives were like a stage play with extensive blocking to make sure we stood in the right places and said the right things.

This, what was happening in my living room right now, was exactly what I thought a family should be. Talking, laughing, enjoying each other's company, making plans and living life instead of just getting through it.

"This is so exciting," I said with a grin. "But you know what will be more exciting?"

"When we make plans to go to Scotland?" my grandmother asked.

"No...when you tell us more of the story from Scotland."

"Ohh, yes, the story is far more exciting than traveling itself." With a chuckle, my grandmother launched into the next part of her story.

Aunt Rose gasped, stumbling back a step to stare at the portrait. "Evil?"

I nodded, my eyes never leaving it. "Evil," I repeated.

Elias snapped his hands away from the frame, afraid the evilness may seep through his skin. "Will it hurt us?"

"I don't think so," I answered, "but I don't have a lot of information on this sort of thing."

"How do you know it's evil?" he asked.

"Just the vibe I get from it. Along with that changing expression."

Aunt Rose's eyes went wide as she shot me a glance. "Changing expression?"

With my eyes still on the painting, I nodded. "Stare at it for a few moments, but...don't look into those eyes. They can... mesmerize you."

Elias glanced away, unwilling to take any chances, but Aunt Rose eyed the portrait. A second later, she gasped again. "Oh, that's..."

"Incredible and frightening all at once," I answered.

Aunt Rose didn't answer. I slid my gaze to her, my lips parting as I noticed her glazed eyes.

"Aunt Rose," I said, grabbing her shoulder and shaking her.

She wagged her head, rubbing her eyes. "Oh, sorry... that's..."

"A powerful painting," I answered as I slipped the cover over it again so the portrait couldn't mesmerize anyone.

"Who is it?" Aunt Rose asked.

I lifted the sheet a tiny bit, squatting lower to read the name plaque. "Lord Raymond McNeil."

"A name to research," Aunt Rose said.

"I do remember seeing it in Clara's family tree." I turned to Elias. "Do you know anything about him?"

"I don't," he answered with a shake of his head. "But I didn't know much about Clara's research. Just a little, and when she got sick, whatever she told me during that which often didn't make sense."

"Would you mind carrying this portrait down to the living room? I think we may need it and I'm not certain I can carry it."

"Of course," Elias said with a nod.

He lifted the covered painting, leading us from the attic down to the next story. As we walked through the halls, whispers swirled around us.

They soon turned to whimpers, and by the time we reached the lower level, wailing filled the rooms, rattling the walls and threatening to make our ears bleed.

Aunt Rose clapped her hands over her ears, her features pinching from the racket.

As Elias set the painting down in the living room, leaning it against the baby grand piano tucked in the corner, the cacophony of screams reached its peak.

Windows rattled, doors banged open and closed, and thunder boomed outside.

I pressed my hands over my ears, wincing as the horrible symphony continued. Elias, wide-eyed and pinched faced, glanced around the room helplessly.

I hurried to the portrait, pulling the sheet away from it to expose the now-grimacing face to the room.

Immediately, all of the noises quieted. With a hard swallow, I slowly lowered my hands from my ears, shooting my companions a wary glance.

"Seems to have done the trick," Aunt Rose answered.

"Trick, nothing. This portrait...this portrait is frightening the other spirits in the house."

Aunt Rose's features squished. "Do you think it's controlling them?"

I bobbed my head as my gaze floated around the room in search of any glimpse of one of the other spirits. "Yes. I think so. Why, I don't know yet."

"So, in other words," Elias said, "the screaming and carrying on was because we unearthed this portrait. And now, with it exposed, they're all too afraid to come out?"

"Yes," I answered with another nod of my head. "But we cannot allow this to stand. We may need to use this portrait while we search for more information but...we cannot let this man control them for much longer."

"So, what steps do you want to take next?" Aunt Rose asked. "Should we try to search the library or look for more of Clara's research?"

"There's a desk of Clara's. It's in the attic, too," Elias said. *"It may have some of her work."*

"Well," I said, *"perhaps we should camp out up there and see what we can learn."*

Aunt Rose nodded. "I'll grab a few blankets, and we'll settle in up there."

"Wait," I said as she gathered a few of the plaid throws from the back of the chairs, *"let me see if I can cover this painting again."*

I crossed back to it and let the sheet slid down over the face. I waited for several moments, but nothing happened. Perhaps it had only been the initial uncovering of the portrait that had stirred the spirits into a frenzy.

"So far, so good," I said with a deep inhale. *"Let's– "*

My words cut off as I twisted to face the foyer, my eyes going wide. "Hello."

Aunt Rose twisted toward me, her brow furrowing. "What do you see?"

"Spirits. Several of them. All women." Without taking my eyes from them, I twisted toward Elias. "Can you describe Clara?"

"Long brown hair, dark eyes. She had a heart-shaped face with a tiny chin. High cheekbones. Slight figure. "

I nodded to stop him from speaking. "She's here."

His breath caught in his throat as he swayed on his feet, his lower lip trembling. "Clara?"

"I can't," Clara answered, her voice a soft whisper. *"He won't let go of us."*

"Who? Lord Raymond?" I asked.

Wails went up from the women. "No," Clara said with a shake of her head, *"don't say his name."*

"All right," I agreed. *"I won't mention his name or uncover his portrait. Can you tell me more about what happened here? What happened to you?"*

"A curse. A terrible curse. He cursed us all. Each first-born

daughter, cursed to die within one week of their twenty-third birthday."

"But why?" I asked.

"You must find the reason. And find the way to free us. I was close but..."

"You died before you could finish," I said when her voice trailed off.

"I wasn't strong enough." Tears welled in her eyes as her gaze went to Elias. *"Please, tell him I'm sorry."*

"I will, but there is nothing to be sorry for, Clara. You did what you could. And we will finish your work. I won't rest until I help you and all of those with you."

"We were all taken too soon," Clara said. *"All of us loved and lost before we even had a chance to experience our full lives. And he keeps us here. He holds us here even in death."*

"Yes, I know. I'm working to help you, but we haven't had much luck. We– "

"You must help," Clara interrupted. *"Please. We cannot stay here."*

"Yes, but– "

"We must go. He calls to us. We cannot stray too far."

My shoulders slumped, wishing she could stay and guide me further. "I understand. We'll keep working on it."

She and the other girls faded away from my view, leaving behind only an icy chill in the air.

"They are gone," I said with a sigh.

"Did you learn anything?" Aunt Rose asked as I eased into the armchair, my eyebrows knitting.

"Not much. There is a curse. From him–oh, do not say his name, it gives him more power over them."

Aunt Rose nodded as did Elias before I continued. "They are being held here even in death. We must learn the reason for the curse and the way to break it. Clara fell short before she succumbed to it."

"All right," Aunt Rose said with a nod. "Then that's what we'll do."

I reached to my aunt, taking her hand in mine and squeezing it. "Gosh, I'm so glad you're with me. Both of you."

Elias shifted his weight from foot to foot. "I just want her to be free of the pain. Those last few days were..."

Tears shined in his eyes as he failed to complete his statement.

"I understand. We all want that for each of the spirits trapped here." I rose from my chair, resolution filling me. "Well, we know what we need to do. Let's get started."

Together, we climbed to the attic again, allowing Elias to lead us to Clara's desk.

"She said she hadn't learned everything, but maybe her notes can point us in the right direction," I said. "But we'll have to find answers beyond this."

"We will," Aunt Rose said, patting my arm.

As Elias reached for the drawer pull, a loud bang startled us all. I crossed back to the stairs leading down, heat washing over me.

"What is it?" Aunt Rose asked.

I hurried down the stairs and twisted the knob, a sigh escaping me as my head fell against the door. "We've been locked in. We're trapped."

CHAPTER 10

My jaw dropped open as I stared at my grandmother. "Seriously? Who locked you in? The mean ghost or the ghosts that wanted your help?"

She tilted her head, her shoulders lifting toward her ears. "That is the question, isn't it? And good for you for picking up on the idea that it could be either."

"Well, it could be, right? Like sometimes nefarious things aren't as nefarious as they first appear. Maybe they were trying to guide you…just in a really weird way."

The grin on my grandmother's face made me think that stumbled onto something. "You are going to make an excellent psychic witch, Carly."

I smiled at her, pleased that I was already doing well. "Thank you. But…it seems obvious."

"It's not too many people. Many people think anything like this is bad. Any spirit that uses these methods are bad."

"But they're just desperate," I answered. "And they can't communicate well, so they need to guide you in a really weird way. The only way they can."

"That's right," my grandmother said. "Although, the bad ones can do quite nasty things like this."

"I bet it's really hard to figure out what's going on, especially while it's happening."

My grandmother nodded. "It can be, yes. The important thing to remember is that you always need to move forward no matter what happens. It's quite normal to feel scared, even upset, but you must calmly put one foot in front of the other to solve the situation."

I wondered how I'd handle it in the heat of the moment. It was one thing to sit by in a bean bag chair and analyze the situation, but it would be quite another to be locked in a creepy attic and not know if it was a bad ghost or a good one who had done it. "Right, okay. Just…keep trying to move forward."

"That's right. And with that, I think I will move forward to bed. We'll pick up again tomorrow after your painting lesson and maybe a bit of practice with that music box. I'm quite interested to know its story."

I climbed out of my chair, raising my eyebrows. "Maybe you should work on it then? I may be slow."

"No, no, dear. You'll do it. I'll help, but I will not take this opportunity from you. Besides, this spirit seems attached to you. I'm certain you'll do better than I will since she already feels comfortable with you."

I huffed out a breath, surprised she knew so much about this already. "I'm not sure comfortable is the right word."

"She called to you, Carly. That's why you found that music box in that shop. She was calling to you."

My brow furrowed. "How did she…"

"They can sense you. They try to reach out to anyone they can. They are often suffering terribly."

My features pinched as I imagined them waiting for

someone to help them, sometimes for centuries. "That's so awful. I really hope I can help her."

"We will, Carly," my grandmother assured me. "But don't be too hard on yourself. You are still learning. So, it may take some time. But we will help her."

I swallowed hard as I nodded. I knew I'd take it hard if I didn't take to this like a duck to water. This poor spirit needed my help. She'd reached out to me, hoping I could end her suffering. And so far, I'd just been too scared to even start to search for answers.

"I'm going to give it my all."

"That's all we can do," Grandmother answered as she slid a lock of hair behind my ear.

We said our goodnights, and I climbed the stairs, leaving both her and Lester behind. I shut myself in my room with Whiskerina and plopped on my bed.

My eyes fell on the music box, my heart going out to the poor spirit attached to it. I considered reaching out to touch it again but decided against it. I didn't want to mess anything up before my grandmother taught me how to communicate with the spirits.

After another few moments, I changed my clothes and crawled into bed to sleep. When I woke the next morning, the music box was the first thing on my mind.

I had my painting lesson first before I could work on it. And I was dying to hear more about Scotland. I had a full day, so I kicked off the covers and hurried to dress for the day.

When I appeared in the kitchen, my grandmother glanced at me over the rim of her teacup. "Well, you're up bright and early."

"I have my painting lesson, and then I want to start on the music box," I said.

"I love your enthusiasm," my grandmother said as she rose to fix my breakfast.

I waved her back to her seat. "I can make my own."

"Oh, and we're enterprising today, too." She winked at me.

"I want to learn how to cook more. I never learned at home, but you cook stuff I love, so I want to learn how to make it all."

The truth was I wanted to grow up to be just like my grandmother. She was so…awesome all the way around. She helped spirits, she had a completely different outlook on life than most other people, and she was an excellent cook.

I hoped I could turn out at least a little bit like her. I wondered if I'd have a child who would reject me.

"What are you going to try?"

"Eggs? The dippy kind," I said. "Can't ruin eggs, right?"

"Not really, but there is a secret if you want that kind."

I set the pan on the stove and slid my eyes toward her. "What is it?"

"Bacon grease." My grandmother grinned at me. "I always keep it in a jar after I fry it. You'll find it in the door of the refrigerator. Just take a spoonful and put it in the pan and turn it on medium heat."

I followed the instructions, wrinkling my nose at the white lard as it dropped into the pan. "I think you're fooling me."

"I'm not, I promise. Now, let it heat. To test it, get a few drops of water on your fingers and flick them into the pan. If it sizzles, it's ready. Drop the egg in and it will get nice and crispy. And then, just spoon the hot grease over it instead of flipping it, less chance of breaking it."

I did as she suggested and soon had a crispy egg that looked delicious. "I did it."

"You did," she answered as she set a piece of buttered toast next to my egg.

My shoulders slumped. "Ugh, I forgot the toast. So, I only made half my breakfast."

"That's all right, you'll learn."

We settled in at the breakfast bar, and I took a bite of my crispy egg white, savoring it. "Mmm, it's just like yours."

"I told you. Next, we'll try the hot chocolate or something similar."

"Yes, I love that hot chocolate. And those potato things… gnocchi."

"Those are a bit harder, but we'll try those, too."

I tore a piece off of my toast and dipped it into the warm yolk. "I'm nervous but excited to start learning with the music box, too."

"I'm certain you are. It will not be easy, but I'm glad you're so eager."

"When you say it won't be easy, do you mean because the ghosts can be frustrating, like in the stories you tell where they aren't very straightforward with what they need or how to achieve it? Or do you mean because it will be hard for me to get used to communicating with spirits."

After a sip of her tea, she answered, "A little of both, I suppose. They can be confusing, but also, you may find it difficult to seek them when you'd like to speak. It really is very much an art, not a science."

I bobbed my head. "Oh, also, I think I want to be homeschooled. I'm not one hundred percent yet, but…it seems like the best fit to give us freedom to travel if we'd like to."

"Yes, it would do that. All right, when you're certain, I'll begin to plan. And you'll learn everything you would at school and then some. Don't think this will be easier for you. It may be harder."

"That's okay," I said, lifting my chin. "At least I'll be able to learn more."

"That's a good attitude, Carly."

I finished my breakfast, washed my dishes, and left the kitchen behind to work on my painting before my art teacher arrived.

"You're making excellent progress," she told me as she studied my painting. "These details you've put in are so very intricate. Your imagination must be quite good."

I beamed at her before we discussed a few more techniques to clean up my work. After the lesson ended, I walked her to the door before searching for my grandmother.

My stomach had twisted itself into a knot as I anticipated trying to reach the spirit attached to the music box.

I found her sorting through photos in the living room. She grinned as I entered. "All finished?"

"Yes." I glanced at a few of them, my eyebrows pinching.

"I thought you may like to see a few photographs of my trips." She slid a picture across to me of two women standing outside of a large manor house. "Here is Aunt Rose and me at Blackthorn Manor."

"That's you?" I flicked my eyebrows up, surprise on my features.

"Don't sound so surprised, you'll be old one day, too."

"Not that," I said with a giggle as I slid into the chair next to her. "Those pants."

"It was the seventies," she said as I chuckled over the bell-bottoms with wide colorful stripes.

"Yeah, obviously."

"One day, someone is going to chuckle over your skirts and cat-eared hoodies, and you're going to say…but it was the two thousands."

"Probably," I admitted, recognizing my unique sense of style. "And they'll say…Grandma, you had pink hair?"

"Yes, that's right. And they'll laugh and laugh."

We chuckled together as she shared several more photographs before I finally slouched back in my chair, sliding my eyes sideways to her. "So, can we try this music box?"

"Of course."

"Should I bring it down?"

"Let's go to your room. I want you to feel comfortable and relaxed. And also, I want the bed available in case you... have an adverse reaction."

"Adverse reaction?" My nose wrinkled at the words.

"You may pass out or become dizzy. Then I can easily help you to lie down."

"Oh, okay," I said with a nod as we climbed to our feet.

My stomach churned as we ascended the stairs, and my chest constricted. I suddenly felt unsure as I wiped my sweaty palms against my leggings.

My grandmother grinned at me as we pushed into my room.

I offered her an awkward smile back, trying to stop my lower lip from trembling. "So, do I just...like sit on the bed or..."

My grandmother crossed to my nightstand and retrieved the music box and pendant. "Yes, that might be best."

I swallowed hard as I plopped onto the edge, blowing out a shaky breath.

"It's all right, Carly, it likely won't be much different from what you've already experienced. There is nothing to be afraid of, but you don't have to do this if you're not ready."

My heart hammered against my ribs as I stared down at the music box in my grandmother's hands. "I want to try."

"All right," she said. "And I will be right here with you every step of the way. Now, for this time, just focus on the experience. Don't try too hard to glean details, just relax and let her come to you."

"Right," I said. "Relax and let her come to me."

My grandmother inserted the pendant and the music box snapped open. The haunting music played as the mermaid reached toward me. My pulse quickened as I took the music box in my lap.

She placed a steadying hand on my back, gently rubbing.

I blew out another breath as I stared down at the mermaid, trying to relax myself. My fingers trembled a little as I reached for the porcelain hand.

As I made contact, the now-familiar jolt shot through me, but I tried to remain relaxed. I slid my eyes closed, focusing on my breathing as I waited for the spirit to reach out.

An image formed in my mind, a woman floating in water. Her hair splayed out as her dark eyes bore into me.

Bubbles floated from her mouth as she opened it, a greenish hand reaching toward me.

My features pinched as a deep sense of melancholy overwhelmed me. I wanted to cry and scream all at the same time.

It became so intense than I thought I may burst. As her hand brushed my cheek, terror shot through me, coiling my insides into a tight knot. I gasped, choking on the water that filled my mouth.

Panic overcame me as the liquid filled my lungs. I was drowning. I wasn't going to live. I was dying.

I tried to scream, but I couldn't. Thrashing as I searched for the surface, I clawed at anything I could find.

The woman floated closer, her hair tickling my cheek as she whispered a single word in my ear. "Carly."

Blackness formed at the edge of my vision, closing in the world around me until I was gone.

CHAPTER 11

My eyes snapped open with a start, and I flailed around, desperate to stay alive.

"Carly," my grandmother's voice calmly said. "It's all right, darling. Take a deep breath."

A cool cloth pressed against my head as my features pinched and I grimaced, sobs wracking me.

"It's all right, Carly, you are safe."

I finally realized where I was. Not underwater, not drowning, but laying on my bed.

Lester sat on one side, and my grandmother on the other.

She smiled at me as I focused on her face, reaching a trembling hand out to touch her to make sure she was real.

She wrapped her fingers around mine and kissed my hand. "I'm here. You're all right."

"What happened?" I asked, my voice shaky.

"You had a bit of bad experience. You became quite frightened and were gasping for breath before you fell unconscious."

My forehead creased as my gaze flicked outside to the black night sky. "Is it night?"

"Yes," my grandmother answered. "You were out for the entire afternoon."

"What?"

"It's all right. It's nothing to fuss over. I'm certain you're feeling weak, tired, and probably many other things from the experience."

I bobbed my head, the things I'd felt when the spirit touched me still lingering inside me. "Yeah."

"I can leave you two alone to talk," Lester said as he rose.

"No," I answered with a shake of my head. "No, I don't want you to leave."

"All right," he said, returning to his seat. "Whatever you want, Carly."

"I just…I felt all these things. Really sad things."

"Oh, yes. She's a very powerful spirit. I think she overwhelmed you."

"I just…suddenly felt sad and scared."

"Likely the things she felt in life, possibly in her final moments. It can be quite overwhelming, my dear."

Silence stretched between us for a moment before I said, "I'm sorry."

"Whatever for?" my grandmother asked.

"All the trouble. I feel like I really failed."

"You didn't. You made contact. That is excellent, Carly. Frightening for you, but excellent work."

"But I was bedridden for half a day."

"You'll get the hang of it. You will become used to it. This was your first time." She patted my hand.

I bobbed my head. "Right. Maybe next time, I'll be better prepared."

"You will be, but it may still be overwhelming. You'll just take your time, and we'll work through whatever comes."

"How about if we work through a late supper?" Lester

asked. "I'll go prepare it while you get Carly situated in her bed."

"That would be lovely." My grandmother grinned at him before she twisted to me. "Do you think you can stomach some food?"

"Yeah, I'm hungry."

"I have no doubt. Contact burns a lot of calories."

"I'll be right back. And don't start any stories of Scotland without me." He winked as he rose and went to the door.

I snapped my gaze to my grandmother with a slight smile. "Will you tell more of the story?"

"Of course. It will help relax you, I think."

"Definitely," I said with a grin as I shimmied up to sit while my grandmother adjusted my pillows behind me.

Before long, Lester re-entered the room, carrying a large tray filled with cheese and fruits and three frosty glasses of strawberry lemonade. My mouth watered for a taste of the sweet drink.

I gulped down half a glass before I even attempted to eat.

"Cotton mouth?" my grandmother asked before biting into a slice of aged white cheddar.

"Yeah," I answered with a nod. "Is that a side effect?"

"Yes."

I loaded my plate with cheese and fruit, my stomach rumbling. As I popped a grape into my mouth, my grandmother pinched her eyebrows together.

"Where was I in this tale?"

"Locked in the attic," both Lester and I said at the same time.

"Ah, yes, the attic." She nodded before she continued her tale.

We settled into seats around the desk, each of us taking several pages of notes from Clara's research. As I stared at the handwrit-

ing, I wondered if Clara may make a reappearance and guide us in some way, but sadly, I was only left with the papers in my hand.

They didn't detail much beyond the causes of death for each of the first-born daughters preceding her. All of them fell ill suddenly, just as she had.

With a sigh, I shuffled through the remaining papers, but found nothing of interest.

"Has anyone else found anything?" I asked. "Mine has nothing about the man of interest or how to defeat him."

"I have a few on...him," Elias said, waving a page in the air, careful not to mention the man's name.

I retrieved them from him and read the information. It seemed Lord Raymond had a penchant for dark things, and he was a man who liked to get his way. From the little contained on the pages, I was able to piece together a tragic tale.

"It seems," I said to the others, "that...the man...may have brought this on his own house."

"Oh? He angered a local witch?" Elias asked.

"No, I think he set the curse himself. Apparently, his first-born daughter was engaged to marry a Duke. She rejected the match after falling in love with a footman."

"Forbidden love," Aunt Rose said with a nod.

"Yes. He took it quite badly as the Duke's fortune was vast and his connections would have helped you-know-who quite a bit with his business. However, once the Duke learned of her other interests, he quietly broke off the engagement."

"Quietly? That seems reasonable of him," Aunt Rose answered.

"Yes, but the father was not pleased. He railed against his daughter, it seems, and while these pages do not specify it exactly, I'm willing to bet that he, himself, cursed her."

"How awful," Aunt Rose said.

I nodded in agreement. "What's more awful is that we haven't a clue about the curse itself or how to undo it and release their spirits."

With a deep sigh, I set the pages aside and leaned back against the support beam behind me. "If only we had some clue as to what could end this."

"Elias, are there any other notebooks or papers she used to detail her work?"

"Not that I know of," *he answered.*

"She told me that she hadn't found the answer. I'm not certain that will help us. We need– "

A gust of wind cut off my words, but the source of it remained a mystery. My hair blew wildly around as the sheets billowed. Clara's papers scattered, some sticking against the pillars, others being swept into dark, dusty corners.

But as they were blown away, another set of yellowed papers raced by me. My brow furrowed as I wondered where they had come from. I snatched one from the air as it fluttered past, my heart skipping a beat.

"Quickly, grab as many as you can," *I instructed to the others.*

In a mad dash, we scrambled to save as many of the blowing papers as we could until the gust died down.

"What did you see?" *Aunt Rose asked as we compiled our papers.*

"This appears to be written by Eleanor McNeil."

"His daughter?" *Aunt Rose asked.*

"The first one cursed. Perhaps they will give us some clue."

Aunt Rose nodded as she worked to neaten her stack of papers. "Everyone scan your pages, see if there are any clues."

We sat in silence, each reading the words penned many moons ago. Elias was the first of us to speak. "Mine all talk about falling in love. A beautiful tale, but sadly lacking in information about how to save her."

"Mine aren't much more informative," *Aunt Rose said.*

With a sigh, I stared down at my crumpled yellow pages. "I haven't found much either, but she keeps mentioning a music box.

And during the first night in the house, I heard the strains of one. I'm wondering if that has something to do with it."

"You never found the source, though, did you?" Aunt Rose asked.

"No." I shook my head. "No, I didn't but it cannot be a coincidence. I propose we search for the music box. If anything, perhaps it will empower the spirits to help us a bit more."

"It can't hurt, and we're not finding much up here." Aunt Rose grimaced. "But we're stuck."

As she said the words, a loud creaking echoed in the attic. I scrambled to my feet and raced to the stairway. "It's open. I'm going to take this as a sign that we're on the right track."

"You could be right," Aunt Rose said as she joined me. "I'm also taking it as a sign that perhaps the music box is not up here."

"I couldn't tell where it was from. Each time I got close, it seemed to move."

Aunt Rose sucked in a deep breath as we descended the stairs with Elias trailing behind us. "Well, where do you want to begin?"

"Ladies, if you don't mind my making a suggestion?" Elias asked.

"Not at all," I answered, "you likely know the house better than we do."

"There is rumored to be a secret passage that leads straight to the heart of the house. I'm not certain exactly where it is, but the entrance is supposed to be somewhere in the billiard room. Perhaps we should start there? Maybe the music box is hidden in the passage."

"That makes sense. It would make it sound like the music was coming from all parts of the house, perhaps," I said.

"Well, it looks like we have our work cut out for us in the billiards room, then. Shall we?" Aunt Rose asked.

With nods all around, we descended to the first floor and made our way to the large gaming area. I heaved a sigh as I scanned the space, searching for a clue to the mysterious hidden entrance to this secret passage.

I hoped a ghost would pop up and tell me where it was, but I had no such luck.

"Any signs that would point us in the correct direction?" Aunt Rose asked, studying my face.

With my lips pressed tightly together, I shook my head. "Not a one. I really had hoped there would be some reassurance that this was the right direction, but the spirits are mum."

Elias rubbed his chin as he studied the space. "It must be on one of these three walls. That one is an outside wall, so it couldn't be there."

"Well, there are three of us. Everyone pick a wall?" I asked.

We selected our areas and set to work searching for the hidden space. My fingers searched every nook and cranny on the wainscoted wall, unable to find any way to open a passage.

With each inch explored, my heart sank a little further, wondering if perhaps we weren't on the right track at all. I'd almost finished searching the wall when my fingers hit what felt like a knot in the wood, yet no knot existed.

My pulse quickened as I explored the oddity, pressing and pushing on it at every angle until finally I heard a clicking noise.

"Ah!" Aunt Rose exclaimed from across the room. "A piece of the paneling has popped open."

"I think I triggered it with this spot on the wall." I poked a finger at the spot I'd used.

"Well, shall we explore?" Elias asked. "I'll grab a few flashlights."

Aunt Rose and I waited the few minutes it took for Elias to bring three flashlights back to the room. I stood at the entrance, the scent of musty air wafting past my nostrils as we prepared to enter, my heart pounding against my chest.

With a hard swallow and a shaky breath, I clicked on the flashlight. It did little to pierce the blackness inside the passage.

My nose wrinkled as I took my first step, a rancid scent filling my nostrils and twisting my stomach. I grabbed onto Aunt Rose for support as my knees threatened to buckle.

"What is it?"

"Something...foul," I managed to choke out. "Something or someone doesn't want us in this passage."

"Then we're on the right track," she answered.

I bobbed my head, though no matter how encouraging those words were meant to be, they struck fear into my heart. We were on the right track, but would it cost us our lives?

CHAPTER 12

"Your lives?" I choked out as I set my glass aside, feeling fortified from the food and drink.

"It was that nasty of a smell. I immediately sensed danger," my grandmother answered.

I wrinkled my nose, trying to determine if a scent had ever warned me of impending danger. "Is that normal?"

"Oh, yes, very," she said with a nod.

"Do you think I'll have that ability?"

"Very likely, yes," she answered.

"And you'd do well to heed it," Lester added. "If you sense danger, prepare yourself."

I nodded at him, though I hadn't a clue how to prepare myself for danger from a spirit. I hoped my grandmother would teach me. A coy grin crossed my features. "Although... these stories are sort of...dull now, right?"

"Dull?" My grandmother sat straighter, fake hurt crossing her features. "My stories are dull?"

"Well, we kind of have a major spoiler. Obviously, you lived."

She chuckled. "I suppose you have me there."

"Not that it's a bad thing," I quickly added. "I'm pretty glad you lived."

"Yes, you wouldn't be here, otherwise," Lester said with a wag of his finger.

I shook my head. "Not just that. I wouldn't have been able to come here after my parents died. And that would have been awful."

"Oh?" my grandmother asked. "I was under the impression you weren't very pleased about coming here, though I certainly understand that. You suffered a terrible tragedy."

"I wasn't," I admitted honestly. "I thought it would be pretty awful here. I was so used to my way of life, I really thought this would be terrible. I also thought you'd hate me."

"Hate you? My own granddaughter?"

"Well, I have the pink and purple hair, the cat-eared hoodies. I'm…different. People don't like different."

"You are more like me than you know," she answered. "Different is not a bad thing."

"It is where I came from. Everyone was supposed to do the same things and act the same way."

"Not here," my grandmother said with a raise of her chin. "Everyone does their own unique thing. And I quite like your pink and purple hair. I think it suits you."

I grinned at her. "And you said I could get some blue, right?"

She bobbed her head. "Or green, though I don't think that would work with your complexion."

I giggled at how easily she talked about it. My parents hadn't been happy but hadn't made me cut off all my hair when I came home from a friend's house with it done. "I don't want any green. But I do want more of this story."

"But you said it was dull because I lived, and you knew it."

That elicited a belly laugh from me. "I said I was glad you lived, but the story isn't dull, far from it. And I can't wait to find out how my music box plays into the outcome."

She smiled at me. "Well, I suppose we can go a little further with the story. Though you must be growing quite tired."

I stifled a yawn, unwilling to show her how tired I was. "A little. But I can stay up a little longer."

"Maybe some ice cream will help," Lester suggested.

I bit my lower lip as I beamed at him and nodded. "I think so."

He disappeared from the room, taking the remnants of our meal with him and returning a few minutes later with a tray of bowls. I eagerly dug into mine, stirring the chocolate and caramel sauce around before I scooped up a big chunk of the chocolate cream.

After her first spoonful of ice cream, my grandmother said, "All right. Settle back into your pillows, and we'll continue."

A chill swept over me, and I shuddered as I took my first step into the passage.

"Cold?" Aunt Rose asked, noticing the goosebumps peppering my arms.

"Yes and no. I imagine you don't find it frosty in here, but I do. There is something odd going on. We're being discouraged from moving forward," I answered.

"Discouraged?" Elias asked as he followed behind us, checking that the passage remained open as we went.

I nodded, my breaths shallow as I fought through the nausea from the sickening smell assaulting me. "Yes. I would say the man responsible for this is trying desperately to stop me from reaching something in this passage."

"I don't feel or sense anything," Elias answered.

"No, I doubt you would, but you may also not feel or sense the

answer when we reach it. It may be quite safe for you to traverse this passage. It is me he resents."

"You hold the power to destroy his hold on these women," Aunt Rose said. "I imagine he's going to put up a fight to keep his control."

I nodded, letting my shoulder fall against the wall as I struggled to move forward. "He's fighting very hard."

Aunt Rose wrapped her arm around my waist, helping to steady me. "If you need a break, just let us know. We can go back out."

"That would only make things worse. I'd have to traverse all of this again."

She nodded, her lips pressed into a thin line. "But if you start to get worse, I'll take you out myself."

I huffed out a quiet chuckle, trying to add levity to bolster myself. "Do I look that bad?"

"You look a little green around the gills," she admitted. "Pale, clammy."

I winced, wondering if this was a normal reaction. "I wonder if Mom ever had this."

"She suffered terribly on some of these cases," Aunt Rose admitted. "Fevers, nausea, weakness. Just like you're experiencing. Not always, but some of these spirits were buggers."

"This one is."

Elias shoved his flashlight toward Aunt Rose. "Take this. I'll carry her. You tell me when to go and stop."

Before I could protest, I was swept off my feet. It did little to help the lightheadedness I was experiencing, but at least I didn't have to worry about collapsing as I walked.

"Okay, move forward. I sense something, but we're not close enough yet. I imagine when we do close in on whatever it is we're searching for, we'll know."

Elias bobbed his head as he continued down the passage with

Aunt Rose leading the way, her flashlight working hard to piercing through the blackness surrounding us.

The walls began to rattle around us as we continued. A roaring growl made my ears hurt, and an icy wind blew past us.

"We're getting closer," I shouted to my companions over the din.

"Yes, we must be," Aunt Rose answered. "Even we are beginning to experience what you are. The icy cold, the terrifying noises."

"The smell," Elias said, his nostrils flaring.

"I can walk," I said.

"It's not turning my stomach. Smelled worse spreading manure. No, you just tell me when to stop."

With a nod, we continued down the passage. The assaults on our senses didn't cease until we rounded a corner, snaking behind the dining room.

Without warning, all of it stopped. An eerily silence pervaded the space as ice crystals formed on the walls around us. I reached out to touch one, wondering if it only existed in my mind, but the ice melted as soon as my warm fingers touched it.

"What's happening?" Elias asked. "Some sort of freeze here?"

"It's him," I explained. "He is literally trying to freeze us out."

From the silence stretching between us as we inched forward, one noise split the air. A quiet tinkling played slowly.

"The music box." My heart skipped a beat before racing faster. "It must be close. We must find it."

"There's another branch in the passage ahead." Elias paused when we reached it. "Left or right?"

I closed my eyes, trying to search for the sound of the music. "Left."

He nodded and took a step to the left when a burst of heat reached us.

"Where is that heat coming from?" Aunt Rose asked as we pressed forward, the sudden change in temperature a surprise.

Sweat beaded on Elias's brow as he lumbered forward with me in his arms. "Maybe from a heater—"

His words cut off as we rounded another corner in the labyrinthine passage. Flames crackling, eating away the wooden slats forming the walls and curling toward the ceiling. Heat from the fire wafted toward us along with heavy smoke. My throat, nose, and eyes burned from it.

Aunt Rose's eyes went wide, and she gasped before spinning to stare at us. "Fire! We need to get out of here!"

"I'll go to town for help," Elias said as he spun on his heel and hurried away from the passage.

Every instinct in me screamed to go back for the music box, but the fire prevented us. Something about it didn't seem right to me, though. The way the flames licked the ceiling, but it never caught fire, the lack of charred materials on the floor from the burned wood slats.

"Wait, wait," I shouted.

"What is it?" Aunt Rose asked as we hurried along.

"Stop!"

"No," Elias answered. "We can't stop. We'll be burned alive in here if we're trapped."

"No, we won't be," I assured him. "I believe that fire is mere trickery. Another barrier trying to stop us from finding the music box."

"That music box may be important, but not more important than our lives," Elias answered. "We'll find it later."

"Put me down. I'm going back for it."

"Are you crazy?" he asked as he continued forward.

I kicked my feet, pushing against him. "Put me down. You can leave the passage, but I assure you there is no fire."

"Put her down," Aunt Rose instructed, her features pinched with confusion, but curiosity dancing in her eyes.

Elias set my feet on the ground with a shake of his head. "I think you're nuts. I can see the fire with my own two eyes."

"You see what you think is a fire, but it doesn't behave the way a fire should."

"I'm pretty certain fire doesn't behave. That's why it's so devastating." He shook his head. "You two women want to take your chances, go ahead, but I'm going to town for help."

"Fine," I answered with a nod, preferring him to leave. It would be easier to deal with the angry spirit without any additional victims for them to use against me.

He pushed past us and retreated down the hall. I twisted to face Aunt Rose. "If you prefer to wait here– "

"No," she said with a shake of her head. "I trust your instincts. Let's go investigate."

With a nod, I slipped my hand into hers, and we rounded the corner, inching our way closer to the fire blazing in the hall. "Notice how it looks exactly the same as it did before."

She nodded as she studied it. "And there is no more damage to the walls."

"Correct. A fire raging like this would be spreading by now."

"You have a point," a gruff voice said from behind us.

I turned to find Elias hovering in the passage, a frown on his face.

"I thought you were going to town."

"I was...until I thought better of it. Didn't want to leave you two ladies in a burning building. Plus...I was intrigued to see if you were right."

"And you think I may be?"

He crept closer, eyeing the fire. "Maybe."

One corner of my lips tugged up as I lifted my chin. "All right, let's continue our investigation then."

We crept closer, the heat burning my skin and sending waves of doubt through me. Perhaps this was a fire. Perhaps the timber around it hadn't caught yet because of some treatment or perhaps the flames were eating away at an area we couldn't see.

I glanced at the floor, finding no ashes or charred remains of anything.

My eyebrows pinched as I struggled to make sense of it. "I can feel heat, yet...nothing else is adding up."

"Is it heat?" Aunt Rose asked. "Or the perception of heat?"

I snapped my gaze to her, my mind working through the implication. "In other words, I think I should feel heat, so I'm feeling it?"

She nodded. "Yes."

"Well, there is only one way to find out." I stretched my hand out, coming closer to the flames.

If I wanted to determine if the fire was real, I'd have to stick my hand into it and risk injury to prove my point.

I sucked in a shaky breath as I hesitated, fear coiling inside me. Was I about to make a huge mistake?

CHAPTER 13

My eyes went wide as I quickly lowered my gaze to my grandmother's hands. I hadn't recalled any signs of a bad burn on them, but maybe after years, the scars had faded. Or maybe she had been correct, and the fire had been a figment of their imaginations, designed to scare them.

She quickly slid her hands behind her back, a coy smile on her lips. "Searching for evidence?"

"Yes," I admitted.

"Well, at least I've left you on a cliffhanger that you don't know the ending to." She grinned at me as Lester chuckled.

"She got you this time."

"Aw, Grandma!" I protested. "Tell me more."

"I think we'll wait until tomorrow. You can barely keep your eyes open."

"I can too," I answered, widening my eyes to prove it.

"You have yawned more times than I can count in the last moments of that story. And I know your energy is quite low given your encounter earlier. You need rest. Particularly, if you want to try again."

I slumped my shoulders as I settled back into my pillow. "Fine."

I was exhausted. And I did want to try to reach the spirit again, but I'd never be able to do it without some sleep. I didn't know much about connecting with spirits, but I could tell that already just by instinct.

"Good. Then you get some rest, and we'll continue this tomorrow."

"After I try with my own spirit."

My grandmother bobbed her head as she rose from her chair and dragged it back to its spot near the window. "And this time, we'll be prepared for any adverse reactions."

She approached the bed again and leaned over to kiss my forehead. "Sleep well, darling. If you need anything, you know where to find me."

"Good night, Carly," Lester said with a smile. "Get some rest."

"Thanks."

They left me behind, and I settled into the silence of the room, allowing it to surround me as I went over the details of my grandmother's story along with the burgeoning mystery I faced in my own psychic journey.

Too many questions crowded into my mind, and I craved sleep to escape from them, but I couldn't bring myself to turn off the light.

Now that I knew all of these tales were real, now that I had experienced this world on my own, I suddenly found myself afraid.

I swallowed hard, clutching a stuffed animal closer to my chest as my eyes darted around the space in search of threats. If spirits could make you think your house was burning around you–or actually start a fire–maybe I didn't want to go any further.

Fear made my thoughts race in a nonsensical way, and I

found myself imagining one frightening scenario after another.

Tears stung my eyes. I'd likely be a disappointment to my grandmother. She was so brave, and I was a coward. My lower lip trembled as I sought the courage my grandma had displayed at such a young age.

As I considered pulling the covers over my head to hide from any spirits that could be lingering in my room, a quiet knock sounded at my door.

My pulse sped, my stomach twisting into a knot. Had a spirit come to torment me already?

"Carly?"

The sound of my grandmother's voice steadied my heartbeat, and I blew out a sigh of relief. "Yeah?" I called out, trying to force strength into my voice but failing.

The door opened, and my grandmother slipped inside. "Still awake?"

"Yeah, just...thinking."

She offered me a knowing smile as she crossed to the bed and eased onto the edge. "Care to share?"

I shook my head, hoping in the dim light she couldn't tell that I'd been on the verge of tears. "It's nothing, just...you know, thinking about the story."

"And perhaps your own experience?"

I chewed my lower lip, again, trying to find the courage to not be afraid.

"I came back because I was concerned that you may be a bit anxious. It can all be very overwhelming."

I puffed out a breath, wondering how she could always read my mind. "I guess I was. Actually, I was afraid."

I lowered my gaze to the duvet covering me, embarrassed by my own cowardice.

My grandmother took my hand and patted it. "That's nothing to be upset over. Fear is a very healthy thing."

I furrowed my brow as I snapped my gaze to her face, lit by the moonlight streaming in my window. "I thought fear was a bad thing? People always say to face your fears."

"Yes, people do say that, but fear isn't bad. Fear is what keeps us alive in many cases. Fear is healthy, if you learn how to listen to it but not let it control you."

"Huh?" I licked my lips as I tried to sort through how I'd give in to my fear but not let it control me.

"When the hair's stand up on the back of your neck, you should heed that, Carly. It's a warning of something. Prepare for it. But do not be driven by it so that you act nonsensically."

"Oh," I said with a nod. "I think I get it."

After another quiet moment, I added, "I think I was being nonsensical before you came in. After realizing they are all true, those stories are kind of scary."

"In a way, yes. But you don't need to hide under your bedcovers and tremble. Facing spirits can be challenging, dangerous, frightening, but you *can* face them."

"I hope I can," I answered. "I'm afraid I'll be scared. And I'll be a disappointment."

"Carly, you could never be a disappointment to me."

"What if I wimp out and don't want to be a ghost whisperer or whatever?"

"That's your choice," my grandmother answered. "There is nothing wrong with that. It's a challenging occupation. It's often frustrating. It can be daunting, difficult, and dangerous."

I wrinkled my nose at the words.

"It can also be very rewarding."

"Doesn't sound like it."

She gave me a knowing smile. "Well, take your ghost for example. The one tied to your new music box. She's desperately reaching out to you. Do you imagine it will feel rewarding if you are able to help her?"

I considered it, imagining this spirit tormented for years, then finally set free before I nodded. "Yeah, I guess so. I mean...I'd be one of the few people who could free her from the pain she's in."

"Exactly. But it may be very scary and difficult. Like an onion, we will have to work to peel back each layer until we find the truth and use it to help her."

"And that will take time and courage."

With a soft smile, my grandmother nodded. "Not everyone has the patience for that."

I pressed my lips together, my features scrunching. "Well, I'm not very patient, but I can try."

She laughed as she patted my hand. "You will learn patience. I did."

"I thought you were just naturally like this."

"Definitely not," she said, her giggle turning into a belly laugh. "We'll navigate this together. And you never need to be embarrassed to share what you're feeling."

"Okay," I said with a nod. "A lot of times, I just think you'll think I'm weird or bad."

"That will never happen. Your emotions are valid. And I am here to help you sort through them. If you feel scared or upset, you can tell me. These cases can take a toll, especially at your young age. You may find yourself overwhelmed with sadness, and I'd rather you tell me than suffer alone."

"Okay, it's a deal. I'll tell you."

"Good. Now, what do you say about a sleepover?"

The words made me break into a smile, and I shimmied over in my bed to make room for her. "Yeah, let's do that."

I felt one hundred percent better having another living person in my room. I figured my grandmother knew enough about spirits that she could help me navigate any creepy sightings. With her lying next to me, I fell asleep in minutes, exhausted from my earlier experience.

When I woke, bright sunshine streamed into my windows, and I found a note telling me to come down for breakfast when I was ready.

I eagerly climbed from my bed, ready to take another stab at my own ghost again as well as hear more about the story.

I hurried to get dressed and head downstairs for my breakfast. The sweet smell of Belgian waffles filled my nostrils as I entered the kitchen, finding Lester sipping his coffee as my grandmother tended to the waffle iron.

"I thought I heard you up," she said as she lifted a golden-brown waffle from the steaming griddle and slid it onto a plate.

"There are strawberries, whipped cream, and syrup," she answered as she set it in front of me.

My mouth watered as I dropped a dollop of the sweet cream on top followed by fresh strawberries.

"How are you feeling today, Carly?" Lester asked.

"Better. The sleep really helped. And I'm not going to wimp out today. I want to try again with my spirit."

"All right. Well, let's get some breakfast into you first," my grandmother said. "And then we'll talk about it."

"I'm still on the edge of my seat over your cliffhanger," Lester said, narrowing his eyes at her hands over the rim of his coffee mug. "I've been studying your hands for a clue."

"Have you now?" My grandmother chuckled at him as she playfully tossed the end of a dishtowel at him. "And what have you concluded?"

His brows furrowed as he puckered his lips. "Well, I don't see any scarring. Your skin is smooth and soft. I think you were correct. The fire was an illusion."

My grandmother raised her eyebrows, but otherwise gave

no indication about whether or not he was correct before she shifted her gaze to me. "Do you have a guess?"

I studied her hands, too. "I did the same thing as Lester, but you have really nice skin, so I think you were right, too. You usually are."

"Well, that *is* a compliment. My granddaughter thinks I am usually right. I'm told by the other grandmothers that their grandchildren usually think they are always *wrong*. We are just old fuddy-duddies who, despite our years of living, have managed to remain vapid."

"I don't think that," I said with a wrinkled nose.

"You're right to think that, Carly. Your grandmother is very wise. Listen to her."

"And Lester. You are very knowledgeable."

I glanced at him as he shook his head. "I have nothing on you, Althea."

"Actually, I think you're both pretty smart. So, I'll listen to both of you," I answered.

"A good decision, Carly." My grandmother patted my hand. "Well, I suppose I owe you both an answer."

My grandmother sucked in a breath and raised her eyebrows as she prepared to continue her story.

My fingers lingered in front of the leaping flames as I steeled my nerves. I'd insisted that the flames were not real but when faced with the prospect of proving it, my stomach twisted into a tight knot and my heart hammered against my ribs so hard, I feared it may break them.

Before I could touch the fire, Elias grabbed my arm and tugged it away. "Wait. Don't stick your hand in there."

"But I have to," I argued. "I really do believe it is not real, and I need to prove it."

"Aye, I understand that. And we will prove it, but...I'll be the one to do it."

"No!" I shouted with a vehement shake of my head. "No, I can't ask you to do that."

"You're not asking, I'm offering," he answered. "And besides, if you believe what you say is true, I'm in no danger."

"Yes, but if I'm wrong…"

"You'll burn your hand something terrible. Better a crusty bugger like me get a bad burn than a pretty, young woman such as yourself." He twisted to nod at Aunt Rose. "Same goes for you."

"That's a ludicrous reasoning, and you know it. No one deserves to get burned."

"Maybe not, but I can't in good conscience let either of you do this. I'll stick my hand in there and see what happens."

I swallowed hard as I tried to think of an argument to dissuade him but fell short. "I still can't agree to this plan."

"You don't have to." With the words spoken, he reached forward, sucked in a deep breath, and thrust his hand forward.

My heart leapt in my throat when his flesh pressed into the flames. He immediately yanked his hand back, and I assumed he'd been burned.

"How bad is it?" I cried as I searched his skin for the blistering that would soon bubble up.

He stood dumbfounded, his features pinched. Was the pain that bad that he couldn't speak?

"I…I'm not burned. I can't believe it, but I'm not burned." He twisted to face me, a grin spreading over his face. "You were right, Althea. You were right."

I matched his expression before I turned toward the fire and slid my hand into one of the dancing flames. Nothing burned my skin. In fact, an icy coldness surrounded my hand as I forced myself to hold it steady.

"Amazing," I said with awe as I marveled at the illusion.

"So, we should be able to proceed past this point without harm…at least from the flames," Aunt Rose said.

I bobbed my head before I squared my shoulders and walked

right through the wall of flames. When I reached the other side, I spun to face them. "It worked. Let's keep going."

Aunt Rose nodded before she followed in my footsteps with Elias coming behind her. We left the fake fire behind and continued down the passage.

The slow, tinkling music continued until it became so loud it almost broke my eardrums.. I clapped my hands over my ears as I continued forward, my features pinching in pain from the loud noise.

As I rounded yet another corner, something glowed at the end of the passage. I slowed my steps as I approached it, cautious but eager to determine if it was the music box creating the racket.

Closing the gap between myself and the object, I found the mahogany box on a pedestal. With the lid open, the haunting melody filled the air.

The rich velvet interior contrasted with the raven perched on a thick oak branch, spinning in graceful circles.

I eased the lid closed to stop the music from playing when the entire house shook underneath us. With my legs braced, I glanced around in search of the source.

"Play the music, Althea," a whisper said. "You must play the music."

I sucked in a sharp breath, recognizing the voice as that of Clara, but I failed to understand her meaning. The music box had been playing intermittently already, and it hadn't stopped the attacks. How would I change anything?

CHAPTER 14

"And this is the music box that I have, right?" I asked as I dried my plate and put it back into the cupboard.

My grandmother shut off the water and grabbed a dishtowel to dry her hands. "Yes, it is."

"Now I'm really curious to know if it did change anything. It looks really cool. I like the raven inside and the song, but…that just seems so…absurd."

"Absurd?" she asked.

"Yeah. I mean…really? After all these years, a music box is going to counteract this evil spirit?"

My grandmother chuckled. "You would be surprised what can counteract spirits. There are so many nuances to this."

"Speaking of," I said, shifting my weight from foot to foot, "should we try with my spirit again?"

"That is entirely up to you, Carly. We don't have to push it. If you're not ready, you could work on your art. That's very soothing and can help bolster your abilities."

I crinkled my nose. "Really? Art can help me as a psychic?"

"Art relaxes your mind and allows you to funnel your emotions in a positive way. So, yes, it can help you tremendously."

"Wow, I hadn't realized that. But it makes sense, I guess. When I'm painting, everything else seems to fade away."

"Yes, I have very much the same experience. I'm looking forward to getting back to it. I haven't painted in several weeks."

"Because of me?"

"No, because of me," she answered. "I needed time to adjust to everything that has happened, and I chose to spend more time with you than with my painting."

I felt needy, suddenly, as though I'd ruined my grandmother's quiet life.

"Don't read into it, darling. I have plenty of time if I would like to paint. I've chosen to do other things."

I brightened. "Like plan our road trips. We still need to plan the next one to Phoenix Hall."

I froze, a wince crossing my lips as I snapped my gaze to her. "Oh, sorry. We can skip that one if you'd rather."

"Why would I rather?" she asked.

"Well, your mom…" I left the words dangle in the air between us. I wouldn't want to go back to the place that had been responsible for my mother's death.

"That was a very long time ago, dear. And I have already been back there, remember."

"I know," I said, recalling the tale she'd told me about the place. "I thought then it was someone named Emma, but it was really you. So, I'd understand if you didn't want to go there again."

"It's all right, Carly. I'm fine going there. So, we'll plan our next trip for Phoenix Hall. Now, would you prefer we worked on that, or did you want to try connecting to your spirit?"

I sucked in a deep breath. "Spirit. That way, we'll still have something to talk about if I pass out again and have to spend the rest of the day in bed."

My grandmother laughed again before she nodded. "All right. But I hope you don't pass out this time. I have some strategies I want you to try."

I raised my eyebrows. "Strategies?"

"Yes," she said as we climbed the stairs and headed for my bedroom. "Now, these may not work. You may have a more difficult time connecting to the spirit or you may not be able to do what I am asking. I don't want you to fret over it."

"Okay," I answered as I perched on the edge of my bed, my gaze falling on the mermaid music box. "What are they?"

"The last time it seems the spirit dragged you into a vision, a very frightening one. Is that right?"

I recalled the sensation of floating in water. "Yes. She...I was underwater. I thought I was going to drown."

"Yes, the spirit is calling you to her rather than the opposite. This time, I want you to let her come to you, but resist her pull. I know that sounds confusing, but if she tries to take you somewhere, resist her."

"Won't she get mad at me?"

"She may. Or she may give up, or even become despondent."

I tugged my lips into a frown. "I feel bad for her."

"Yes, I know." My grandmother eased onto the bed next to me and smoothed a lock of my hair back behind my ear. "But we cannot help her if you are relegated to your bed for the better part of a day after every encounter."

I licked my lips. "Right. Good point."

"If she does manage to take you underwater again, or anywhere else frightening, I want you to remember the part of the story I've just told you with the fire. None of it is real. It's all an illusion."

"So…I can't drown, right?"

She shook her head. "No. You aren't even near water. You are only perceiving that you are in water. It's a vision, nothing more. Nothing you see can harm you."

"Okay," I said with a deep inhale. "Okay, I think I'm ready to try."

She smiled at me before she kissed my forehead. "You are a very brave young woman, Carly. Remember that. And very compassionate to want to help this spirit."

I beamed at her, proud she thought that much of me as she rose and retrieved the mermaid music box. After unlocking it, the haunting tune filled the room, sending a shiver down my spine as I anticipated the upcoming encounter.

"Whenever you are ready."

I chewed my lower lip, memories of the last time shooting through my mind and clouding it. "It's not real," I whispered to myself before I reached a shaky hand toward the mermaid's fingers.

A jolt shot through me as my fingers touched hers. Water bubbled around me, but I resisted her pull. "You come to me," I said into the blackness that surrounded me.

"Carly," she whispered.

"I'm here, but you come to me. I can't come to you."

"Carly," the voice called again. "Follow me."

I shook my head. "No. I want to help you, but I won't follow you into the water."

Details filled in the blackness around me, and I found myself standing on a rocky shore. Waves crashed below me, and a light swirled at the top of a lighthouse that jutted into the stormy sea.

Panic rose within me as I wondered where I was and how I could get back home.

"Follow me, Carly," the voice said again.

"Tell me your name," I insisted.

A form materialized in front of me, a woman, her wet hair clinging to her pale cheeks. I stared at her, hoping to get an answer, but instead, she disappeared.

"Wait!" I called before the image faded away.

"Wait, wait!" I called again, but when I opened my eyes, I found myself lying on my back in my own room.

My forgiving mattress wrapped around my body as the familiar sights and sounds of home filled in around me.

"Welcome back," my grandmother said.

I tried to sit up, but found the room spun when I did. With a sigh, I slumped back into my pillows. "Did I pass out this time?"

"No, you remained conscious. So, you have taken a step forward."

"I didn't follow her," I said. "But she didn't want to talk."

"I am not surprised. You are both testing each other's boundaries. It will take time."

I sucked in a breath, frustrated by the situation. "It never seemed like it took this long for you to make a connection."

"I am different from you, Carly. And I was in different circumstances. Being in the place where the spirit stays or died is different from channeling through an object they have attached themselves to. Are you able to talk about your experience or would you like some time to mull it over?"

I swallowed hard, the experience still lingering in my mind. "I can talk about it. I'd rather."

"Okay, when you're ready."

I was in blackness, and I could hear a voice calling to me. I told her I wouldn't follow her, but I wanted to help her."

"Very good. Setting the spirit at ease is an important part of our work."

"Suddenly, I was on a coastline. There was a lighthouse, and the sea was stormy. She materialized in front of me, and I asked her name, but she left. That was it."

"Very good," my grandmother repeated with a nod. "That's excellent work, Carly."

"I don't feel like I learned very much."

"Ah, you learned lots of things."

"I didn't even get her name. I may be able to sketch what she looks like," I answered. "Maybe. At least her eyes. They are so…pleading."

My grandmother smiled at me. "They often are, yes. But, while her name is an important part of the story, you've learned something about her location. Seaside, a lighthouse. Was the coast rocky or sandy?"

"Rocky," I answered.

"Would you recognize the lighthouse if you saw it?"

I shrugged. "Maybe. They all look alike."

My grandmother chuckled as she patted my hand. "Many of them do, yes. However, not all of them. We'll have a look if you make no more progress, all right?"

I bobbed my head as I finally rose up to sit, the room steady. "At least this time I didn't pass out."

"I told you that you would make progress faster than you expected."

"Still doesn't really feel like progress. I feel like you would have solved this already."

My grandmother shook her head. "I doubt it very much. Channeling is not my strongest suit. I can do it, though not well."

I screwed up my face. "Somehow, I can't imagine you being bad at anything."

She chuckled as she patted my hand. "Well, you will far

surpass me at channeling based on what I've seen so far. Especially with your commitment to helping the spirits."

I grinned at her. "I hope I get good at it. I want to be as smooth as you are with them."

"It's not always a smooth process. And you will make many mistakes, but it is very rewarding."

We sat in silence for a few more moments before thunder boomed outside. The kitchen door banged shut as the rain chased Lester into the house. His footsteps sounded on the stairs a moment later, then a knock on my door.

"Come in," my grandmother called.

He peeked through a tiny crack. "Everything all right?"

"Yes, she did quite well today. Stayed conscious the entire time."

"Well," he answered with a grin as he opened the door further, "congratulations. And here I was all prepared to make another cheese plate and serve it to you."

"I wouldn't turn it down, but I can help this time."

I climbed from my bed, feeling a little tired, but much better than after my first experience, and we headed downstairs to make a light lunch as the rain pounded the roof.

We spent over an hour planning our next road trip. With Lester planning to join us for the drive to Phoenix Hall, we debated different routes, looked at various inns and hotels, and mapped out our first day.

As we wrapped up our discussion, I prompted my grandmother to continue with her tale. "Come on, it's perfect weather for it. And it sounds like we're getting toward the end. This music box *has* to have something to do with it."

"Oh, you think it does, do you? Well, let's see if you are correct," she answered with a grin before she launched into her tale as we huddled by the fire and the storm raged on.

My hands swept over the polished wood of the music box, sending a jolt through me that I hadn't expected. I yanked my arm back, rubbing my fingers where it had touched me, but there was no visible mark.

"What is it?" Aunt Rose asked. "Have you gotten any clues from the spirits?"

"No, just a shock," I answered.

"Shock? Must be a buildup of static," Elias said as he reached toward the box. "Seems to be gone now."

I carefully placed a finger on it before withdrawing it and shaking my head. "No, it's not. This isn't static electricity, it's something else."

I twisted to face Aunt Rose. "Did Mom ever mention anything like this?"

"Not to my knowledge, however, she didn't do a lot of channeling which is what I think is happening or what the spirit is attempting."

"Channeling?" *I repeated.* "No, I don't recall much information on that in Mom's journals."

I studied the polished wood box, my eyebrows knitting. "Looks like I'm on my own."

"It doesn't seem to affect anyone else here, just you," Aunt Rose said. "I could carry it out of here, and we could regroup in the living room."

I sucked in a breath as I nodded. "All right. I'll have to tackle it at some point, I think, but we can be more comfortable outside of this space."

"Right," Aunt Rose said as she reached for the music box. *She yanked on it, her brows knitting as she stared down at it.*

"What's wrong? Did it shock you, too?" *I asked.*

"No, but..."

"What is it?" *I asked.*

"It's stuck." *She tugged on it again but couldn't lift the small music box from the pedestal on which it sat.*

"Stuck? It can't be," Elias groused before he reached for the item and tried to lift it.

It didn't budge. Elias scratched his head as he ducked to study it. "Must have some sort of glue or...paste."

He slid his hand around the edge before he tried to pry it loose from the pedestal with a fingernail. "I can't get it."

"Let me try again," Aunt Rose said. "My nails are longer, maybe I can get a start breaking whatever has sealed this to the pedestal."

She traced the rim with her thumbnail but made no progress. "Nothing. It's like nothing is holding it except I can't budge it."

Elias shook his head. "I can get a few tools. Pry bar should work."

"All right," Aunt Rose agreed. "Althea, do you want to wait here or go with Elias?"

I didn't answer for a moment, my mind whirling before I reached toward the box. "Just a moment. Let me– "

My fingers touched it, and the shock shot through my body again. I struggled to control my mind but managed to lift the box easily.

"You've done it!" Aunt Rose exclaimed. "How?"

"I'm not certain," I said my voice shaky as thoughts and images bombarded my mind. "Maybe I'm the only one who can handle it?"

"Maybe," she answered. "Well, let's get you to the living room. Once there, maybe we can–"

"Please hurry. I'm losing my vision," I answered.

"What?" Panic laced her voice as she placed a hand on my arm. "Althea, put the box down and see if it resolves."

I wanted to, I wanted to drop the box to stop the assault on my senses, but I couldn't manage to do it.

"I'm not sure I can."

Aunt Rose placed her hands around it and pulled, but the box remained stuck in my hands as though it had been glued to my fingers. "I can't budge it."

"Let me try," Elias said, wrapping his thick fingers around the box and tugging. With a grunt, he finally released the box and shook his head. "I can't move it. What is happening?"

"I believe I am channeling something, but I'm too green to know what I'm doing. My vision keeps going in and out. It's like I'm seeing the past, like I'm immersed in it."

"Is it giving you any clues?" Aunt Rose asked.

"Clues?" Elias shot back. "We don't need clues, we need to stop this from happening to her."

I shook my head. "I'm not certain we can. And it may be for the best. This may be—"

My voice stopped, and no matter how hard I tried, I couldn't get it to work.

"Play the music box." The words came from my own mouth, but I hadn't said them.

"Althea? Did you get a clue."

"This isn't Althea. You must play the music box." I struggled, able to hear everything going on, but blind and unable to speak.

"Who am I speaking to?" Aunt Rose asked.

"Clara. You must play the music box."

"Oh, Clara," Elias said, a sob in his voice.

In another moment, the sensation passed, and I collapsed to the floor. Aunt Rose dropped down on a knee next to me. "Althea?"

"Yes," I said, sucking in deep breaths. "Yes, it's me. I'm back."

"We spoke with—"

"Clara, I know," I said with a nod. "I could hear her, but I couldn't see or speak. This is very odd."

"Can you walk?"

"I think so," I answered.

Aunt Rose slipped a hand under my arm and Elias did the same on the other side. They hauled me to my feet, careful to keep hold of me in case I collapsed again.

My knees wobbled, but I managed to move forward, the music box still clasped in my hands. We snaked through the secret *passage toward the opening. My mind clouded several times, but I remained in control of my own faculties.*

When we emerged in the billiards room, I collapsed against the table, relief coursing through me at having escaped the passage. But my comfort was short-lived. Before I could suck in a second breath, the floor beneath my feet began to shake, producing a rumbling so loud it nearly made my ears bleed.

"The ceiling's going to come down!" Elias shouted as a loud crack resounded.

Before we could move, it split in two and a chunk rained down, smashing a hole into the floor.

With a cry, I tried to move, but my limbs were weak and slow. Aunt Rose grabbed hold of me and tugged. As we made our way from the room, seeking safety, I wondered if we would make it or become the house's next victims.

CHAPTER 15

"Wow," I said as Lester added a few logs to the fire behind me and poked at it. "You were channeling, just like me?"

"Not quite like you. It was a little less…structured. Plus, you seem far more adept at it than I was."

"But you were thrown into it head first. Like sink or swim. I may not be adept at it at all had you not helped me." I stroked Whiskerina's fur as she yawned and stretched, awoken by the fire's loud crackling.

"You show a tremendous talent for it, help or not. I've no doubt you would have figured it out on your own. Your natural curiosity is another plus for you, Carly."

I grinned at her. "Really? Mom and Dad always told me it was nosiness and would get me in trouble one day."

"It may," she said with a chuckle, "but I am to have you prepared for that trouble as best I can."

I sat stroking my cat's fur, my brow crinkling. "Did… Mom and Dad know about…"

"What I am? Yes," my grandmother said with a bob of her head. "Yes, they did. They did not accept it."

My heart sank as I snapped my gaze to her, my lips parting. "They didn't?"

"Sadly, no." Remorse seemed to float in her eyes. "They preferred to ignore the supernatural."

"How could they do that? It's so obvious it exists. And those spirits need our help."

"Yes, they do. And I'm pleased you are open-minded about it, but…many people prefer to ignore it. Lots do not even know it exists, and those who do don't understand it. When people don't understand things, they often prefer to ignore them, push them out of sight."

I struggled to hold back the tears that filled my eyes. "They would have rejected me."

"Possibly not," my grandmother answered.

I glanced up at her with glassy eyes. "They rejected you!"

"I am not their child. When one's child does something, it's amazing how our perspectives can change. I believe, though, they thought if they kept you away from me, you wouldn't exhibit any of this behavior on your own."

I furrowed my brow. "Would I have?"

"Hard to say. You have a strong talent, so maybe. You may have stumbled upon it on your own, or you may have shoved it away, buried it because of what the world told you was normal and right."

"I'm really glad that didn't happen. I mean, I'm not really glad Mom and Dad are gone, but…I want to help these spirits, and it would have been a shame if I wasted my talents."

"I quite agree," my grandmother said. "Now, what about some dinner?"

Lester chuckled. "That I quite agree with."

"Yes, your stomach has been rumbling for over an hour," Grandmother answered.

We climbed to our feet and made our way into the kitchen to make dinner, all of us pitching to help.

As Lester worked on the salad while I boiled gnocchi, he asked, "Have you learned anything from your spirit, Carly?"

"Not much. She wouldn't even give me a name."

"That's not true," my grandmother said as she worked on the dessert for after our meal. "Carly learned a great deal. We talked about discerning details that aren't obvious, didn't we?"

"Oh, right," I said with a stir of the boiling water. "I didn't get her name, but I did see her. I'll probably sketch her out. Maybe that'll help."

"And…what else?" My grandmother raised her eyebrows at me, prompting me to continue.

"And…oh…I learned she's by the sea, I guess. I was on a rocky shoreline, and there was a lighthouse nearby."

"What sort of lighthouse?" Lester asked.

I shrugged. "I don't know. Just a lighthouse."

"Carly thinks all lighthouses look alike."

Lester chuckled at the words as he tossed the salad with a light dressing. "They don't, you know?"

"They do to me."

"Not to me," he answered. "I happen to love lighthouses. Each one is unique in one way or another."

"Maybe you can help me figure out which lighthouse this is."

"Possibly. Can you give me any details about it?"

I closed my eyes, trying to picture it in my mind. "Ummm, it was tall and white with black stripes. And it had a little white house behind it."

"White with black stripes," he murmured. "All right, I will look for one with that description, and together, we'll see if we can figure out where this may be."

"That's very helpful, Lester," my grandmother said. "I think pinpointing the location will allow us to do some research, and maybe help us glean some other details before we visit."

"Visit?" I asked, my stomach clenching. "You mean...you think we should go there?"

"I very highly doubt you'll be able to help this spirit from here. It is often necessary to visit the location where they are actually trapped."

I licked my lips, unsure I wanted to do that or that I was ready for it. "But…"

My grandmother froze as she closed the refrigerator, her brows knitting. "What is it?"

"I don't know. I don't feel ready for this."

She broke into a smile. "None of us are, darling. But I will be with you every step of the way. And we won't go until you are ready."

I bobbed my head as I fished gnocchi out of the water, still uncertain how I felt about it. I'd honestly never expected to go to the site and do what my grandmother described in her stories. I wasn't even certain I *could* do it. "I hope I can help her."

"Of course, you can. And, as I said, we won't go until you feel ready. But I don't think it will be as bad as you are expecting."

I shot her a glance, a mix of amusement and disbelief. "I don't know. Your stories are pretty scary."

"They can be, but it can also be a little exciting...if you let it be."

I pressed my lips together, trying to find the prospect of being bombarded by ghosts exciting. I guess in a way, it was. The visiting new places and searching for information seemed appealing. Maybe it would be fun to pursue it.

"Well, I think everything is ready for dinner. Shall we eat and finish my little story?"

"Yeah," I said with a grin, the words pulling me from my

rumination. "I can't wait to see if my little music box saves the day."

"You are about to find out," she said as we settled at the table with our meal.

Aunt Rose dragged me into the hall as dust and debris crumbled from the ceiling in the billiard room. The music box remained stuck in my hands, my fingers tight around it as though they were glued.

She took a step toward the front door when a large beam smashed down in front of us, preventing us from moving toward it.

My heart skipped a beat as I stumbled back a step. The floor continued to shake underneath us as Aunt Rose rushed forward toward the downed beam, searching for a way around it. "Maybe we could crawl underneath– "

Before she could finish her statement, the house shook so violently, we were knocked off our feet.

"Aunt Rose," I cried, sending her scurrying toward me to help me up, "I don't think we're meant to leave."

"But...it's too dangerous in here."

Elias nodded as he clung to the wall. "The roof could cave in at any moment."

"The house isn't going to let us leave. In fact," I answered with a hard swallow, "I think it's leading us somewhere."

"Where?" Aunt Rose cried, her voice shrill with panic.

"Not to the front door, that's for sure," I said as I eyed the beam blocking our way.

I twisted to face the opposite direction. "We were obviously ushered out of the billiard room, so we'll try down the hall."

Aunt Rose's lower lip trembled, but she nodded, sliding her arm through mine as I took a tentative step forward.

Nothing blocked my way, though the groaning of the walls continued around us. We crept forward, our eyes searching for threats that could make the home our final resting place.

As we approached another hallway, Aunt Rose tightened her grip on my arm. "Which way?"

I scanned each direction, one of them leading to the ballroom, and the other leading to the library and office.

With a shaky inhale, I nodded toward the office. "Maybe this way? I'm assuming that was his office."

She bobbed her head as Elias lingered behind us. I lifted a foot to take a step down the hall when a rough shaking knocked me from my feet again.

"Wrong way, I guess," I said as I scrambled up to stand.

"Ballroom?" Aunt Rose suggested.

Heat washed over me, and I nodded. "Yes. Yes, I think so. The ballroom is where I had my ghostly dance. I'll bet that was a clue."

"Coupled with the music box clue on the first night, and your inability to let go of it, I'll bet that's where we need to go."

I nodded. "Yes, I think so."

Elias swallowed hard, his hands shaking. "I don't know how you ladies figure these things out, but I sure hope you're right."

"There's only one way to find out," I said, my eyes lingering down the hall at the doors leading to the ballroom. "Let's go."

Carefully, we picked out way toward the double doors leading to the grand space. Howls and shrieks accompanied us as we inched closer and closer.

"Are you sure this is right?" Elias asked as a screaming, icy wind whipped past us.

"I think so," I answered, shouting to be heard above the din. "This is quite common for spirits to act this way when we are close to the end."

He frowned, his eyes scanning the hall for any of them as we reached the doors. They blew open in front of us, beckoning us to come inside.

As I stepped over the threshold, everything stopped. Silence reigned, and I held my breath as I crossed to the center of the room.

"Play the music box, Althea," a hushed voice whispered.

"Here?" I answered. "I must need to play the music box here for it to have any impact."

My fingers finally loosened around the object, and I set it in the middle of the floor before I lifted the lid.

The soft tinkling music poured from it as the rumbling of the house ramped up again.

"I think you may have been wrong," Elias answered as I joined him and Aunt Rose near the door.

I shook my head. "No. No, this is right. This music box has something to do with the– "

My words cut off as I spotted something materializing near the mahogany box. "Do you see that?"

"The mist?" Aunt Rose asked. "Yes."

"What mist?" Elias said, his features squashing.

Before I could answer, a figure formed, the shape of a man. My heart hammered against my chest as I wondered if I was seeing the form of Lord Raymond McNeil appearing in front of me.

Based on his old-fashioned clothes, I would have guessed yes.

"It's a man," Aunt Rose whispered as I bobbed my head.

"Yes, I would expect its him."

"Who has brought this here?" he bellowed as he searched the room.

Several of the female spirits appeared, their heads bowed, and their hands clasped as though penitent.

"Who has brought this here?" he boomed, making them tremble.

I stepped forward, my features taut. "I have."

His red eyes bore into me as he snapped his gaze to me, his eyes traveling up and down my form. "You? Who are you? Answer me, girl."

"I am Althea Ravenspell. And I am here to help these women."

The house shook more after my statement, as though a challenge to the words.

"Help them?" he spat before a low chuckle escaped him.

Any humor on his features disappeared, replaced by a sneer as his red eyes bore into me. "I won't let that happen. I will destroy you like I destroyed them."

The threat hung heavy in the air, the challenge set. One of us would not escape this house. The question was: which one?

CHAPTER 16

My fingers curled into fists as his threat hung between us, but I would not back down.

Instead, I lowered my chin, prepared to do battle with him, using whatever methods I had at my disposal to defeat him.

"What's happening?" Elias shouted from behind us as wind whipped around the room, howling and screaming like a banshee.

"He is trying to flex his authority over me and the others. I won't allow it."

"Fight, Clara," he shouted. "You must fight!"

The growl that emanated from Lord Raymond set the hairs on the back of my neck standing on end. "Your precious Clara will be the first I make an example of."

He reached a gnarled hand toward the woman, dragging her toward him like metal to a magnet.

I raced across the room, determined to stop him from harming her. "Leave her be!"

"Stand aside!" he shouted, waving a hand in the air.

My feet left the ground as he did so, and I flew through the air, slamming into the wall and slumping down to the floor in a heap.

Aunt Rose raced to my side to help me.

"I–I'm all right," I murmured, more concerned about the spirit across the room.

Elias joined us, helping me to my feet. As soon as I regained them, I stormed across the room toward him, but I met such resistance in the form of wind that I could barely move forward. My hair blew straight back behind me, and the pressure on my skin I feared would leave me bruised.

"Let her go!" I demanded as his fingers wrapped around Clara's throat.

The sight incensed me, and I fought through the wind to reach him. I reached out, my trembling fingers making contact with his spirit.

A jolt of electricity shot through my body, followed by a strange prickling sensation.

He twisted, his features pinched as he stared at the odd connection.

"Yes," I said with a satisfied grin, "I can interact with you, too."

My hand traveled down his arm until I began to pry his fingers away from Clara's skin. As I pulled one away, he'd clamp another tighter.

After a few attempts, I gave up on this course, rethinking my plan.

His sinister chuckle grated on my nerves, an indication that he believed he had won. But I wasn't quite finished yet.

I took a different course of action, hooking a finger in his mouth and tugging him backward. The action took him by enough surprise that he released his grip on Clara, who scurried back toward the other women.

He grabbed my arm, the pressure enough that I worried he'd break my arm and threw me aside again.

"You think you're so clever," he snapped. "You are not. And now, I will break you, too. You will become one of my servants."

Another burst of icy wind assaulted me before a burning sensa-

tion filled my body. I cried out as it intensified, feeling like my body would burst into flames at any moment.

As the agony continued, a thumping began in my brain, and before long, a voice sounded—his voice. "Rise and close the music box."

Every fiber of my being wanted to follow the command, but I resisted, digging my fingernails into the parquet wood floor as I fought through the various levels of the attack.

"Rise and close the music box."

"Fight him, Althea!" Aunt Rose called from across the room.

The man snapped his angry gaze to her before he sent her spiraling across the room and smashing into the wall. She slumped to the floor, unconscious.

Elias hurried to her side, pressing two fingers against her neck. "She's okay," he reported.

"But she won't be unless you rise and close the music box."

"Why?" I asked through clenched teeth.

"It disturbs me," he answered. "I hate the sound of it."

The information emboldened me. "Then you will listen to it until I remove you from this world."

"You will not survive until then." He sneered at me, and the pain in my body shot to a new level.

My breathing turned ragged as I desperately tried to fight through the pain I felt. My features pinched as wails went up through the women he'd trapped over the years.

I shifted my pained gaze to them. I had to fight. I had to free them.

My mind searched for a way to stop the pain, but it seared every nerve inside of me.

"The pain can end...simply rise and close the music box."

I gritted my teeth, fighting my strong urge to race to the thing and slam the lid shut. My chest constricted and my heart beat so hard, I thought it might break my ribs.

My mind searched for a way to end it, but instead, I found something else. I recalled the fire in the secret passage. Frightening, but merely an illusion.

I wondered if the pain I was experiencing was also an elaborate deception, something he planted in my mind.

I worked to reassess my pain, manifesting visions of cool breezes whispering through spring trees and gentle water lapping at my feet. Slowly, the burning sensation that had gripped my body diminished, until finally, my heart returned to normal, and my breathing slowed.

With my newfound calm, I rose to my feet, my eyes locked onto his. His eyes continued to pierce my brain, urging me to close the music box.

I fought him as I crossed toward it. The grin on his features broadened as I reached for the object, but instead of closing it, I lifted it in my hands.

"Close it!" he shrieked at me.

My fingers shook as they tried to follow his orders, but I held firm, raising my chin as I shook my head. Instead of snapping the lid shut, I shoved the box forward, dumping it into his hands.

He stared down at it in horror as it continued to play its tinkling music. The walls and floor shook, an outpouring of his fury. "Noooooooo!" he shrieked, throwing his head back.

His outburst threatened to make my ear drums bleed. The other spirits shrank back, frightened by both his frantic screaming and the physical manifestations that accompanied it.

"Now, Althea! Banish him now!" Aunt Rose shouted.

I glanced over my shoulder and nodded before I focused on him again. "Now, it's time for you to go."

In his weakened state, he couldn't fight back. As the music box continued to drain his energy, I said the words to send his spirit where it deserved to go.

"By the power of light and ancient lore, I banish you forevermore. Begone from this place, dark spirit of yore, return to the shadows to roam nevermore."

His features twisted with fear and loathing as he set his eyes on me for the last time. Before he could speak another word, light burst from inside of him, tearing him apart from the inside out until he finally burst into a cloud of pieces.

The force of the explosion rocked the entire room, knocking me from my feet. I fell onto my backside, my eyes squeezed shut from the burst of bright light.

When I finally opened my eyes again, I found the room almost back to normal. A group of women stood in front of me, their features no longer pinched with fear and anguish.

"Thank you, Althea," Clara said, a slight smile playing on her lips. "Thank you."

"You're welcome."

I received more expressions of gratitude until each soul floated away to their eternal existence. Only Clara remained, lingering for another moment to lay a hand on Elias's shoulder. His lower lip trembled as he stared at his jacket, as though sensing her.

"Goodbye, my love," she said before she, too, left the space behind.

Bright sunshine flooded the room as the darkness lifted from the entire house.

I climbed to my feet and hurried to Aunt Rose's side to help her up. "You did it," she said with a smile.

"No, we did it," I answered.

Elias staggered a few steps away from us, peering into the hall. "It can't be."

"What is it? I asked, joining him.

I peered down the hall, finding it devoid of any damage.

"There was a beam across the hall just a moment ago. What happened to it?"

"I believe that was all merely part of the show," I answered. "The house is restored now, back to the peace it once knew before the curse."

He sucked in a sharp breath as he shook his head.

"You shouldn't have any trouble from here out," I said. "And if you didn't know, Clara is now at peace."

Tears formed in his eyes as he bobbed his head. "Thank goodness for that."

Aunt Rose wrapped an arm around me. "Good work. Another set of souls saved."

"And now, on to the next," I answered with a slight smile.

I sat straighter as the story came to an end. "Wow. You must feel so accomplished once you do something like that. Is it amazing?"

My grandmother leaned back in her chair, tenting her fingers as her eyebrows knitted. "I suppose it does."

"I think it would. I mean… you just saved all of those spirits."

"In the moment, I suppose I just think about how many more are still waiting for my help."

I bit my lower lip. "Like my mermaid."

"Like your mermaid, yes."

I cast my gaze downward, tracing the outline of the plaid on my skirt. "I want to help her. But I think I have some work to do first."

"A little bit, yes. We need to know more about where to find her."

I shifted my eyes to Lester. "Can you help?"

"I'm going to try."

With a nod, I answered, "I'll try to sketch both her and the lighthouse. Maybe it'll help us identify it. And then maybe we can plan a trip there."

"Are you ready for that?" my grandmother asked.

"Were you ready for any of it when you started?"

She chuckled and shook her head. "Heavens no."

With a shrug, I nodded. "Then what am I waiting for?"

She grinned at me. "You are a very brave girl, Carly. And you are definitely a Ravenspell."

I smiled back, pleased she had said it, and ready to begin my own adventures while I learned more about hers. If I could save even a fraction of the souls she did, I'd have done something worthwhile with my life.

I couldn't wait to get started. I couldn't wait to have a story of my own to tell. And I would start with my mermaid.

Ready for Carly's first case? Can she discover more about the spirit she'd connected with? Find out in *Wicked Whispers*.

Let's keep in touch! Join my newsletter and receive five free books!

ABOUT THE AUTHOR

Award-winning author Nellie H. Steele writes in as many genres as she reads, ranging from mystery to fantasy and allowing readers to escape reality and enter enchanting worlds filled with unique, lovable characters.

Addicted to books since she could read, Nellie escaped to fictional worlds like the ones created by Carolyn Keene or Victoria Holt long before she decided to put pen to paper and create her own realities.

When she's not spinning a cozy mystery tale, building a new realm in a contemporary fantasy, or writing another action-adventure car chase, you can find her shuffling through her Noah's Ark of rescue animals or enjoying a hot cuppa (that's tea for most Americans.)

Join her Facebook Readers' Group here!

SERIES BY NELLIE H. STEELE

Cate Kensie Mysteries
Shadow Slayers Stories
Lily & Cassie by the Sea Mysteries
Pearl Party Mysteries
Middle Age is Murder Cozy Mysteries
Duchess of Blackmoore Mysteries
Maggie Edwards Adventures
Clif & Ri on the Sea Adventures
Shelving Magic
Whispers of Witchcraft

Made in United States
Cleveland, OH
20 June 2025